NOSEDIVE

by

M.H. VESSEUR

NOSEDIVE

A Radio Detective

A novel by

M.H. Vesseur

Vibes Publishing

Published by Vibes
www.mhvesseur.com
www.facebook.com/MHVesseur

Second edition
ISBN 978-94-91908-28-6 (paperback, 2nd edition)
ISBN 978-94-91908-03-3 (epub with DRM)
ISBN 978-94-91908-29-3 (epub with DRM for Apple iBooks
and Kobo)

Nosedive

One

Aurora Borealis, the Northern Lights, radiates and pulsates and puts up a fine show whether there's an audience or not. If we happen to be looking the other way, it still shines its green light in the long arctic night. But it's hard for us to take our eyes off it, because the sight is spellbinding.

Therefore it's probably worth mentioning that inside the small aircraft, flying high above some snowbound northern country, none of the passengers were paying any attention to the green aerial waves outside the small cabin windows. There were only two passengers — but still.

They were sitting in the luxurious interior that resembled a Manhattan penthouse more than it resembled an airline passenger cabin. The machine was large enough to carry a hundred passengers or more, but it had been modeled as a private jet, with seats for no more than four people, and separate rooms with a bed, a kitchen, a bathroom, a gym and an office with a small conference room. Towards the nose of the plane was a wall of wooden paneling and a door that led to the entrance area. From there, one could either exit the plane through one of two doors on either side of the aircraft or climb a small stairway leading up to the cockpit. The two passengers were alone, surrounded by privacy and the luxury of soft chairs, a bar and drinks cabinet, a flat screen, some large tropical plants and a couple of paintings, all bathing in a soft light coming from the ceiling.

The two passengers were engaged in conversation to a point where it had made them oblivious to the outside world. The green, pulsating light could be seen clearly through the small windows, but they had eyes for nothing but each other.

That is to say: the young man was looking at the girl without interruption. The girl was looking out the window, but without seeing the Northern Lights. She looked at the young man's reflection so that she could avoid looking into his eyes.

And she had a good reason to do that: his gaze was intense. His dark eyes seemed to be glowing like a dying fire, but it was a cold fire. There he sat, in the luxurious leather couch, all bent forward, his hands clutched together, now wringing them, now banging a fist into a palm. His half-long hair, black and shining, moved back and forth with his upper body, a nervous beat to an inaudible music. His white suit, meant for more optimistic times, looked ridiculous now, both to himself and his girl.

His life was not that way now. Had there been any brain capacity left that allowed clear thinking, he might have gotten up and changed into some darker clothes for his thin, muscular body. Black clothes, in particular.

For his girl had just dumped him.

Dumping one's boyfriend on board of an airplane is not necessarily a good idea. There is not enough space to walk away from anything. But the girl had the best of intentions. Her name was Catherine Gretta and the plane was not hers; it belonged to her lover's father. She didn't need a rich father because she had the looks one needs to find one's own fortune. A rich husband would come in handy at some point in her life, but she was too young to forego other options, such as a career in the movies or the fashion industry. Not that any of that mattered now. She was kicking him out for other reasons.

There she sat, in her tight blue blouse and skirt. She wore a hat so large and blue and fluorescent that it seemed to be competing with the Northern Lights outside the window. Its size put some distance between her and the young man, who was becoming increasingly angry. Her long brown hair hung down without movement, shielding part of her face from him.

She now regretted ending their relationship on board the plane. It seemed like a good idea when it first came to her: being able to convince the young man while they were in a confined space that he could not get out of, which offered no distraction from what she had to say. But she had underestimated the impact of her message: that they had no future together (which they hadn't), that she could not live with a man so possessive (which she couldn't) and that he needed to see a therapist (which he did).

Did I actually believe I could convince him of all that? she thought. What kind of fool am I?

He was beginning to scare her.

The pilot and his navigator, also co-pilot, were looking at the Northern Lights when the steward entered the cockpit. He was dressed in a meticulously white uniform.

"Funny how that never bores me," said the navigator. "It's a nice break from the everyday routine stuff."

"Aurora *bore*-ealis," said the pilot, and chuckled.

But he got no response; probably because he had been making that same remark for the past ten years every single time he flew this route. Everybody was used to it by now. And not only that, they would be anticipating that same joke for the rest of their lives.

"Well, down there it's far from boring," said the steward. "Daddy's boy is getting all worked up over something."

The two men in the seats turned heads simultaneously.

"What do you mean 'worked up' precisely?" said the pilot.

"It's starting to sound like a fight," mumbled the steward. "It's rather embarrassing. I was going to do the bedroom, but I didn't want to go in. I think I'll wait a while."

"I'm not sure I agree with you there, pal," said the pilot. "They're kids, basically."

"Rich kids," said the navigator.

"Exactly. Who knows what happens when they get into a fight. They been drinking?"

"No. Well, not much anyway."

"Using?"

"No. They're not that kind. Anyway, I would have smelled it."

The navigator turned to his console to deal with some new numbers, withdrawing himself from the conversation.

"Can you be more precise? Are they raising their voices?"

"What are you worrying about? I wish I hadn't mentioned any of this," said the steward, irritated. "You're getting paid to steer this piece of..."

"Wrong, buddy. I'm getting paid for everything you can think of when it happens on board. Go back down, check them out and report back with an assessment. People can do crazy things when high altitude and claustrophobia and the sight of the Aurora Borealis get to them."

The navigator turned and smiled. Then he winked at the steward, to relieve him of some of the apparent pressure from the chief.

"Whatever," said the steward.

He went out and didn't even slam the door, but that was about as relaxed as things were going to get from here.

The steward wanted to barge right into the living quarters of the aircraft, but once again he halted at the cabin door. The shouting was unavoidable. Obviously the owner's son was completely losing it.

To be honest: he had lost it before. The boy was simply not all that reliable and had a fit every now and then, but the last one had been a couple of years ago and the steward had forgotten about those days, about how they had all been thinking "that boy's not right" and how they had been sure he would end up in an institute. That's how things go with adolescents: one moment you think they're going to the top of the world, the next you don't know what to think.

The steward couldn't hear all of it, but he tried to and he tried very hard. It was all up to him now: if the billionaire's son was going to flip, blow off the lid and do something drastic, the only person who could intervene would be him, the purser. So he listened like his *life* depended on it — which it did, but he didn't know that.

All he could hear were phrases and fragments, and as the girl didn't scream back he could only conclude that whatever she said, it fueled his fire. That didn't strike him as odd: the girl was a very diplomatic young woman, but even her talent for calming some hothead was inadequate for the occasion.

"You cheating liar," shouted the young man.

"..."

"Who cares what your intentions were? Who cares that your intentions were *good* when you kick me out of your life out of the blue?"

"..."

"How can you say that after all this time? You didn't say it, no, you never said anything, but you sure acted like it. You... You..."

"..."

"Shut up! Shut! Up! Please say no more. You gave the distinct impression that we were a couple, that we were in for the real thing and..."

For the first time, her voice was audible above his.

"Even if you haven't noticed, I was very much in love with you, Fernando. But you never want to talk about any doubts I might have," she yelled. "Well, your strategy of ignoring everything that could be painful has brought us here. Not *everything* is up to you, you know."

"You lying bitch," the young man shouted. "You twist and turn everything. All this time and I don't recall you ever saying anything. And now you want to dump me out of the blue. Well, I cannot let you get away with that. Oh no."

The ensuing silence worried the steward. He pressed his

ear against the cabin door and heard the young woman crying. It was the thumping sounds that scared him. Was he beating her up?

"Damn..." he mumbled. Then he straightened his back and grabbed the door.

But it was jerked open and the steward stared into the wild face of the young man.

The only thing the steward could think was: he has gone mad.

Then it all happened very fast.

The door to the cockpit was jerked open before the pilot and the navigator could get up to check out what the shouting was all about. The young man entered the small space of the cockpit and was all over the pilot before the two men knew what was going on.

"Stop him, get him off me!" shouted the pilot.

Then there was turmoil all around. The navigator jumped forward in an attempt to get his hands on the young passenger, but he was kicked in the face by an elbow with such force that he slammed back towards his own seat. Next to him, the steward and the young woman entered. The young passenger slammed the pilot's head against the dashboard, time and again, with an awful force, while he pushed the wheel and they could all feel the plane starting to descend and then make a nosedive. It was horrible and they all felt their stomachs trade places with other internal organs, and they all lost their balance violently.

"Stop it," screamed the young woman.

"No Catherine, no!" shouted the young man. "No! If I can't

have you, no one will. We're going out of the blue, into the blue."

His final words, before the purser hit him on the head with a heavy briefcase, were: "Screw you all!" Then he was on the floor, and silent.

Unfortunately, so was the pilot. Blood had covered part of his face and he lay slumped across the helm and the controls. The navigator, another bloody mess, grabbed the second helm and started to bring the plane back to its original horizontal position.

This all happened quickly and bumpily, as the plane was diving at a sharp angle and roaring down in the night.

The navigator pulled the helm and pulled and slowly the plane started to correct its steep decline, its engines roaring with anger.

"What have you done to him?" yelled Catherine. She held her hands in front of her mouth in shock, momentarily distracted from the real troubles ahead.

"Are we safe?"

"Not yet," said the navigator. "We're too close to the ground!"

No one saw anything in the pitch black before them. There was only the vague lights of the Aurora Borealis in the distance, but it was so high up and behind a mountain ridge that they all knew instinctively that the plane was still going down and that it was already too close to the ground.

The navigator jerked the wheel and the plane turned to the right sharply and there it was: the thin line of a highway in the snowy landscape. It was lit scarcely, but that was enough.

"Get it up!" shouted the purser. "Can't you get it up?"

"Too late... I'm going to try and make a slide on that road..."

The young woman fainted.

Decades later...

Two

The aircraft appeared out of nowhere, as if it were suddenly released by the low hanging clouds. It sailed down towards runway #7, the one reserved for special flights, its chromium nose up in the air as if it wanted to show every living thing on the airport: here I come.

Hitomi Sakamoto stood behind the glass wall of the arrivals area and looked at the machine, trembling and roaring as it touched the runway with its wheels. The arrival of her boss, the host of business talk radio show The Boardroom, also known as "the bizz jockey", was supposed to have been delayed considerably due to the snow storm of the past twenty-four hours, but everything proceeded as scheduled. The storm had lifted a couple of hours ago, the airport crews had cleared the runways and it was business as usual again.

There is an aura of luck around that man, Hitomi contemplated in the midst of the usual airport turmoil, people running and standing around by the hundreds, announcements echoing through the halls, the shouting and running of children. Almost everybody I know has been delayed by the snowy weather of the last couple of days. Everybody, except Mr. Carl Evangelos Pappas. How can that be?

It wasn't often that Hitomi was in a position to actually contemplate her boss. There was a dreamlike quality to the whole scene: her not hearing the immense noise around her, her seeing the aircraft descend in slow-motion from the snow-filled clouds, gray and heavy, and low, almost as if they were lying on top of the buildings surrounding the airport in the distance.

But it was true: Hitomi Sakamoto, producer of The Boardroom, was usually in state of flux, as if she were a planet permanently rotating around an imaginary sun, working round the clock, never stopping for anything. She only stopped if she was forced to, like at this very moment, when she was simply awaiting the bizz jockey's arrival and had nothing else to do. She had made all calls she had to make and could not think of another thing to do, so she had decided to just stand there.

He is a unique man, she thought.

Then her cell phone buzzed.

The plane had touched down and was taxiing towards the building.

"Sakamoto."

"Don. Boss in yet?" the familiarly sloppy voice of The Boardroom's sound engineer Don Wozniak sounded.

"Don Lech Wozniak," Hitomi said, as she snapped out of her dream sequence. "Is it so hard for you to pronounce a full sentence instead of just stammering some words? Listen to yourself: boss-in-yet. Man has acquired the ability of speech over thousands of years and you have the ability to undo all of that in a single line."

"Are you through, miss samurai?" said Don. "If you're nice, I'll water your banzai tree for ya!"

Hitomi uttered a sigh loud enough to draw attention from the people around her. "That's bonsai, Wozniak. Don't make me take you through the difference between bonsai and banzai again. Please?"

"Oh, all right. You win. So he's not down yet?"

"No. And on the way back from the airport I have a whole list of topics to take Carl through, so whatever life-threatening situation you're in, it will have to wait."

"I'm actually on fire."

"Stand under a sprinkler."

"Funny. What if I said it involves you, Hitomi?"

"Call airport security," said Hitomi. "Bye, Don." She saw the bizz jockey through one of the windows, approaching the gate.

Pappas passed right by the luggage belt, as he had once again traveled light.

"I like a man who knows how to travel light," she said to Carl, by way of greeting.

They had a habit of not turning every meeting into a big thing, like everybody else seemed to be doing.

"The whole point of life is that you can't take anything with you when you go, so you have to get rid of everything before your time comes," said Carl Pappas, the bizz jockey. "Women are lousy at that, so men should lead the way."

He walked with his hands in his pockets, without any of the fatigue that stuck to the average airport visitor. Of course, he had made this trip with the WCBN Radio corporate jet. It wasn't too big a plane or anything, but it gave him privacy and some quiet on the way, and a separate gateway to get going much faster. No hassle trying to get out of the plane.

Next to him walked the small Japanese woman, his producer, Hitomi Sakamoto, who had already taken out her tablet and started to fire away at him. Proposals for topics and guests, request from the worldwide business community, management issues to deal with, dispatches from the lawyer's firm that represented WCBN Radio. Carl Pappas' The Boardroom was their biggest client.

An airport security officer, standing still along the side of the huge corridor that led to the car parks, looked on curiously. He wondered if that was indeed that famous radio guy and that if he was, who could the woman be? He thought about how muscular she looked in her fake fur coat, thin legs sticking out underneath, moving with an athlete's stride, and her long black hair spreading over her coat. He wondered about how famous guys always get the young chicks.

Then Hitomi Sakamoto, always aware of everything everybody was doing or thinking or planning in her proximity, turned and looked at him. Her eyes shot a bolt of dark fire in his direction. Then she turned away and she and the famous guy disappeared into the crowd.

No, the security officer thought, she's not that young. Finally, here's a famous guy with a woman his own age.

But boy, that woman must have some abdomen. He could almost...

No, that was ridiculous, he thought. You can't *hear* abdomen. You can't *hear* a six-pack. But then again, if you could, this was it.

Three

The man with the scar appeared out of a curtain of rain. It was pouring down from the gray skies relentlessly, but it made no impression on the man. He might have parked a car somewhere close, and then again he might not. There was no way to tell because the rain made too much noise and limited visibility to a couple of meters.

He felt comfortable under cover of the rain. That way nobody would see him coming or going. He looked around, across the industrial zone, along the many small businesslike garages, importers, air conditioner suppliers and manufacturers. There wasn't a single building with lights switched on and there weren't any cars.

It was a dead zone, but for one small brick building without any windows, with a sign on the front that read: "Doctor Synthetic": the light above the entrance was switched on.

After looking around him for a while he moved forward with sudden haste, grabbed the doorknob of the solid wooden door of the Doctor Synthetic building, pushed it inwards and entered.

Inside, the light was blinding. Fluorescent tubes eagerly shot down their white light, almost as if they were determined to compensate for today's incompetence of the sun.

Now the man was clearly visible. The short black hair that stuck on his head as if it was glued on, all shiny and disorganized. The thick black eyebrows that hovered over his dark, deep eyes. The thin nose and the even thinner lips, that curled as if he was disgusted by something. The broad shoulders under his raincoat that betrayed his muscular body. And finally the scar, an old wound that started right beside his left ear and made a curve across his cheek and landed near the corner of his mouth.

He looked through the building's interior. It was clearly a laboratory of some kind, full of tables with retorts and cupboards stacked to the brim with equipment and folders full of test results and a lot of crates. In the back was a man in a white laboratory coat bent over a table, who looked up.

"Ah, you're finally here. Good. It's all ready for you," he yelled.

His voice echoed back from the ceiling, two stories high.

The man with the scar reached the far end. They shook hands, but the visitor said nothing.

"You're going to be delighted," said the man in the white coat. He walked towards a crate that stood against the wall in the back, and pointed at it. "Here's your order. Wanna check it out?"

The visitor nodded something that looked like "no".

The white coat opened the crate and took out something. He opened his hand and showed a tiny white sachet.

The visitor looked. He took the sachet and inspected it

from all sides. Then, for the first time, he smiled and talked. "Awesome," he said. Then he grabbed a small cart, stuck the shovel under the crate, lifted it from the ground and pushed it towards the front of the building.

The white coat followed. "What will you be doing with it," he asked. "You can do some great stuff with this, you know, create some real havoc with it. Just remember that they go off whenever the surrounding temperature rises or when they're squashed or thrown with force. Basically nothing will happen as long as they're inside the cooling unit in this crate. Just like you said. A fine balance, if I may say so." He clapped his hands. "So, what's it all for?" He winked to the back of the visitor. "You can tell me, I'm not just discrete, I'm secretive with scientific precision."

The visitor pushed the door open with the cart and parked the crate outside in the rain.

"I'd feel better if you tested at least one," said the man in the white coat.

Then the visitor turned and grabbed the white coat's hand.

"You have done well, Doctor Synthetics," he said. "You will get all the feedback you need right here and now."

The two men looked each other in the eye.

The man in the white coat had turned pale all of a sudden, his eyes bulging, looking down at his hand. "What are you do… For God's sake, don't squeeze that!"

Indeed, the visitor squeezed his hand for a moment. Then he was gone, slamming the door shut behind him.

The man in the white coat looked at his right hand. He was holding the sachet. Unintentionally, but he was holding it nonetheless. Only a second had passed since the visitor had stepped outside — but already there was no longer enough time for the laboratory man to kick open the door and throw the sachet outside, or do anything else to save himself.

As the visitor disappeared into the rain, a heavy explosion behind him blasted through the wooden door and shook the stone front of the laboratory. Then, through the hole where the door had been, smoke bellowed out as far as it could. The rain entered the building immediately and started to wash the blood and the body parts off the concrete floor.

Four

"Are you even remotely listening?" shouted Hitomi.

They were in her — Japanese — car, driving to the city. A few hours separated them from the next broadcast of the business news radio talk show The Boardroom.

Carl was driving, and he had just been jerked back to reality as Hitomi had gripped the wheel and corrected a lane change.

"Sorry," said Carl. "I was trying to get around this joke in my head. You know, fix it."

"Oh no," said Hitomi. She was not particularly interested in the part of the show that was supposed to be funny. Of course she laughed, like everybody else, when the bizz jockey aired a great one-liner. But she was the type who could do without; she was the kind of woman who goes to the gym voluntarily. Not to look good or to live longer; only to work on her endurance and her kick-rapists-in-the-crotch skills.

"Why are you driving anyway after a long flight?" said Hitomi.

But the question was ignored in its entirety.

"There's this CEO sitting at a state dinner," said Pappas. "You know, the president's there and some generals are there and all their wives and husbands. The general says: if you would run the country like we run the army, things would go a lot smoother. The president says: if you guys would run the army like we run the country, we'd have less wars and save a lot of money. So the CEO says: if we sell the country to the people, you can both retire."

The bizz jockey inhaled deeply, having told the joke without a breathing pause. Then he looked at Hitomi, who looked at him without even the slightest hint of emotion on her face — although that didn't necessarily mean anything. Keeping a straight face came natural to her: she had an uncanny talent for making the sound of laughter without showing any of the accompanying facial expressions.

But this time she didn't even laugh; although her jaw dropped slightly. "You should ask Job Messner or Don Wozniak, Carl. I'm really not... what's so funny about retirement? LOOK AT THE ROAD!"

Right on time, Carl looked back and was able to avoid bumping sideways into a car on another lane.

Hitomi decided to waste no more time. "OK, it's time for the Boardwalk. You ready?"

The list of program items for tonight's show actually had that title, The Boardwalk, printed on top.

"Sure," said Carl.

He was satisfied with the joke. If Hitomi didn't burn it down outright it was probably usable, although he did want to test it on his staff writer Job Messner and the WCBN Radio CEO Phil Solo too.

"The main dish tonight is Jonathan Grosmont, CEO of the Desi Corporation," said Hitomi. "Remember?"

"Of course I remember, Hitomi," said Carl.

Sometimes he wondered if this was becoming a ritual: Hitomi pretending she had to remind him of who his main guest was.

"The Desi Corporation manufactures desiccants, the little sachets they put in vitamin bottles and bags and computer boxes and sushi blade packages to keep them dry. Billions of sachets travel the world each day. One of the hidden giants of the worldwide economy. As hidden as dry clean hanger manufacturers and container transporters."

Finally, the bizz jockey got his producer's approval in the form of a smile, albeit modest.

"Well done, Carl Evangelos Pappas," she said. "Well done indeed. Anything you want to hit him over the head with?"

"I sure do. Otherwise there would be no point in having him as a guest now, would there?"

This time he was the one who laughed; and very loud at that.

Five

A melody from Johann Sebastian Bach, tortured and made to sound like a ringtone beyond recognition, blasted from the cell phone in the dark of the freight train wagon, and made a dark figure jump up. He cursed. Anger sounded from his voice; he blamed himself for not having taken the phone offline. What if somebody had been close enough to hear this damn' ringtone?

"What the hell are you calling me for?" he snapped into the cell phone's speaker. "I will be incommunicado for another twenty-four hours, I told you that."

The dark shadow lit a cigarette with a lighter, and in the limited circle of its flickering flame the man with the scar appeared.

"If you are so incommunicado, why are you answering this phone?" a man spoke through the phone. "Makes me worry if you're up to the job. Are you on the train still?"

"You got nothing to worry about," said the man with the scar. If I'm not up to it, it's too late now. And yes, I'm on the train." He pushed the door open and looked at the starry sky over the dark landscape. The train was moving fast and there

33

was nobody to be seen outside. In the distance, the only lights came from the locomotive pulling the train, half a kilometer ahead. "I love trains. You ever take trains?"

"I never do," said the voice. "I'm not sure what I hate more: having to be on time, or having to wait."

"But that's precisely the fun of life," said the man with the scar. "You wait till it is precisely the right time for you."

"That is the stupidest thing I've heard in a long time."

"Oh but it's true. This whole job I'm doing for you is all about waiting till the time is exactly right. One move at the wrong moment and my cover is blown. By the way, you're not checking up on me, are you?"

"No."

"Good. I know half my money has been received, so you have nothing to worry about."

"I just called to wish you luck. I've waited a long time for this."

"Ah, you see? You've been doing some waiting too."

The voice through the cell voice sighed. "Yes I did. But a lot longer than you think. I've been waiting for decades for this. So make it good, if you will. Make it good."

Six

In the tax free area of the airport, the man stood in the shop and looked at the backpacks and cases and computer bags. Over his shoulder hung a worn-out bag by its last threads; it was likely to fall down any minute. The weight of the laptop inside had been worrying him for quite a while and he had suddenly, upon leaving the airplane, decided to deal with it here and now. If he was a man who neglected himself — and he was, having allowed himself to balloon up to more than a hundred kilos, developing a bad case of smoker's cough and living under intense scrutiny from his doctor, who had been giving him the cardiac warning — he would not allow his precious laptop to be hurt. His whole life was on his laptop. His social media life, with all the girls in strange countries who believed he was a handsome young man, slim and trained, who lived in a sunny city where movies were made. His business with entrepreneurs and successful business people, who believed he was a digital billionaire who preferred anonymity.

In short: he was not really a man, he was an invention. His own.

But standing here in the shop was very real, and he was sweating, he was tired, his clothes smelled bad and he needed to get to a hotel as soon as possible, to get a bath and some sleep.

"Can I check if my laptop fits in this bag?" he asked the girl at the counter.

"Of course. Shall I do it for you, Sir?" the girl asked, giving him a deceptively open, incredibly white smile.

As usual he was falling for her instantaneously; another habit that had started to deteriorate into an addiction a long time ago.

Not every smile from a pretty face is genuine, he thought. Especially not in expensive shops.

The girl took out the laptop. She looked at the old bag with disgust before she reinstated the smile in all its whiteness. Then she placed the computer inside the new bag.

"Fits like a glove," she said.

The fat man was impressed by her eloquence and pronunciation and slightly hoarse voice. He took out his credit card to seal the deal, while he started shifting the rest of his old bag's contents into the new one. Then he noticed a tiny sachet inside the new bag and took it out to show her.

"I've seen that before. What is it?" he asked.

"It keeps the bag from picking up moisture as it's transported around the world," she said. "That way you can be sure the bag is dry, which is important as you're going to carry your laptop in it. Shall I throw it away for you, Sir?"

The man shrugged, as much a gesture meant for the girl as it was a way of backing off from her beauty. "Hell, no, just put it back in the bag. I'm all for moisture control. You know, what's good for the bag is also good for my laptop."

In a silent way, he hoped the girl would add an impromptu line to that, something like "and what's good for your laptop is good for you!" but that didn't happen of course.

So he paid and walked out of the shop and thought nothing further of the sachet, considering it utterly irrelevant, but that was not the end of the story — although it was almost the end of him.

Seven

By the time the WCBN Radio voice started to announce the daily business news talk radio show The Boardroom, bizz jockey Carl Pappas was beginning to feel the fatigue caused by air travel. Fortunately, he could blindly trust his body to engage every available reserve energy source the moment he needed it — which would be the case in less than a minute. As the trusted announcement of his show burst onto the airwaves and the internet and flowed across the globe, he felt that mysterious force rise.

"Aaaand it's eleven o'clock. The city is dark, but the fire burns. It burns in the offices. It burns on Wall Street. It burns in the City. It burns on the Bund. It burns in Dubai. It burns in the factories and power plants. And it burns within us. Because we are the business and we all need redemption. This is the hour of delusion and today's truth. This is The Boardroom. Here is your prophet, the buddy and the bodyguard of every CEO, the Don Juan of every business babe. Here is the world's one and only bizz jockey. Here is your BJ: Carl Pappas!"

And right then, all his powers were restored.

"Men and women of the business," the bizz jockey said, "welcome to The Boardroom, where just like any other day we ask ourselves: where do we stand? If you know the answer, you may call now. But don't take this lightly; many went before you. Many were mistaken. And are grounded now, in court, in jail or in hell. A few moments from now I will introduce tonight's guest, who is already sweating on the other side of the microphone. And while we wait till our first caller comes in, I have to tell you about this business man who was flying in the company of some extremely influential politicians on board of some government jet."

Beyond one of the studio windows, in the control room, his sound engineer Don Wozniak grinned. Next to him stood the show's producer, Hitomi Sakamoto, and her immaculate appearance only emphasized the sound engineer's sloppy looks. While she stood there as straight as humanly possible, her hair in a knot tied on the scientific center located on the top of her head, a wooden pin pierced through it, a dark red suit that enveloped her gymnastic body like some futuristic foil from NASA, he was slumped backwards in his chair. He was eating the remains of a day-old donut, his blouse partially buttoned, his unshaven belly — this was a feature someone like Hitomi surely noticed with due disgust — peeking out, his black needle-like hair on top of his head pointing in several directions, disobeying all previous orders to stand up straight and form a coherent hairdo.

While grinning, a tiny part of the donut was released onto the console. This only added to the producer's discomfort, while she listened to the joke the bizz jockey was making on live radio. A joke that she didn't get in the slightest and had actually objected to during the editorial meeting.

"He had forgotten to quit smoking at some point in his life and now it was too late. So he was sitting on the plane talking about economics with some of the world's most influential people and all he could think about was his next smoke. So he excuses himself and asks a stewardess if it would be possible to open a window somewhere so that he can have a smoke. But the stewardess doesn't get the joke and she says: 'No, but I can give you something for flying sickness, it will calm your nerves too.' The business man says: 'OK, that sounds good. Where can I undress?' To which she replies: 'Oh, but it's oral, Sir.'"

Soon the first caller came in. As soon as Carl Pappas had delivered the pun, he took it.

"OK, let's hear it."

"Hi Carl, it's Julianne, I'm with a big airliner and I resent all these jokes you make about airline personnel," a powerful female voice sounded. There was sufficient authority in the voice to deal with plenty of opposition.

"Excuse me, Mrs. Airline Big Shot. You caught me off guard there. Am I making jokes about people on airliners more often than about other people?"

Both Don and Hitomi nodded "yes" empathically though with little enthusiasm.

"Duh... my crew concurs. Seems you have a point, Julianne," said Carl. "But tell me, what exactly do you do on planes?"

"I work for an airline, but I'm in the management. My point is, you always talk about how CEOs are on planes and then they get into some kind of conversation and so forth, but the personnel on board is always ignored or ridiculed. As if they're foot soldiers and don't really matter."

"That's because they áre foot soldiers, Julianne. And when their careers are over, they are footnótes. In history. Bye Julianne, fly safe."

He moved his thumb in the air, drawing an imaginary trajectory for a throat cut, and Don Wozniak terminated the connection.

"If that's the average level of tonight's Boardroom, I'll be fired in the morning," said Carl loud. "Please don't talk to me about trivialities. Julianne, you're welcome to call again if you have a topic that makes me choke on my mike."

For a moment, he paused, and then continued: "And now, right after this break, I'll be back with you business people and I'll introduce my mystery guests for tonight!"

And Don Wozniak shoved some buttons and said to Hitomi: "Don't you just looove blindfolding men."

She reacted as if stung by a bee. "That was never my idea. I'm opposed to the whole thing."

"You also never proposed an alternative method, Hitomi."

"It's the only way to keep both guests anonymous to each other right until the moment Carl does the intro... What do you care?"

Don smiled.

Hitomi walked off to get the blindfolded guests and escort them, one by one, into the recording studio.

Eight

"It's Monday night. It's half past eleven. Tonight, as usual for every fortnight here in The Boardroom, is Mystery Hour. Two business big shots. They'll both be facing an opponent they are not expecting. And neither are you. Fifteen minutes. You are all witnesses. Listen to how they react. Listen for the one who keeps a clear head and for the one who abandons ship. Who saves face? Who walks the talk? You decide. Your referee: Carl Pappas."

As soon as the WCBN Radio announcer silenced, the bizz jockey took over.

"I'm very excited about tonight's guests, because they are representing an issue that takes place today and that affects many families. Let's see what they have to say. Please remove your blindfolds, gentlemen!"

There was always a certain amount of tension in the studio during a live broadcast, but the exposure of blindfolded guests to their opponents usually heightened the excitement. For a moment it felt like anything was possible.

And indeed, it was.

The two men had barely been able to keep their hands off

their blindfolds. So now that their time had come, they jerked the cloth off — as one.

"Oh no," yelled one guest, a fortyish man with a beer belly, a balding head, a slightly unshaven chin and large glasses, dressed in a white T-shirt and jeans, with a smoker's complexion.

"That figures," said the other, a man in his fifties, well groomed, wearing an immaculate dark suit over a slim body, an ageing athletic man.

"Well," said Pappas, "you guys may be familiar with each other, but before you start throwing mud across the table please do introduce yourselves to my listeners. There's ten million business boys and girls out there who are dying to find out who you are and what to expect."

"I think this sucks," said the T-shirt guy. "Of all the people..."

"No comment yet, just your credentials please."

"Yeah, OK. I'm John Bremen, I'm foreman at the Desi plant," said the T-shirt guy.

The other guest, throwing his blindfold on the table irritably, said: "It's the Desi Corporation, actually." And then he added: "I'm Jonathan Grosmont, I'm CEO of the Desi Corporation, which includes the factory complex where Mr. Bremen is currently employed."

"Welcome to my..."

But John Bremen, the T-shirt guy, leaning back in his chair, putting on an I-couldn't-care-less air, spoke louder than the bizz jockey: "Yeah, cur-rent-ly, you'd like that, wouldn't you? Well, I got news for you buddy, I'm not going anywhere and the way things stand I might just be working for Desi longer than you."

Grosmont shook his head without showing any other response on his face.

"Good. Góód!" said Pappas, "I like you guys already. I can feel a fire here. Well, here's a short introduction to these two gentlemen's backgrounds. The Desi Corporation has been the target of a large strike at its factory. John Bremen here is leading the strike, which started this morning, and he's also the union man. Jonathan Grosmont is of course the main man for the negotiations, representing management. How are you at diplomacy, Jonathan?"

There was a sigh.

Beyond the window Hitomi's cheeks were glowing, as the coming few moments would determine if this item was going to be any good.

Beside her, Don Wozniak held a finger close to the button that would take the microphones off the air and replace them with a jingle or some music or some commercials.

"I'm disappointed in you, Mr. Pappas," said Grosmont. "A week ago your people invited me to come tonight. This morning a strike breaks out. And guess who is my mystery opponent? Am I the only one here who thinks this is all way too convenient to be a coincident?"

"Grow up, Grosmont. You think I set you up? You and Bremen have been at war for a whole year now, it's inevitable that this would happen. All I knew was that you'd either strike a deal — in which case the both of you would still be welcome on my show to celebrate — or you'd still be fighting over wages and labor conditions. But let's ask Bremen. You started a strike this morning, a couple of hours before this show.

Why's that?"

Bremen suddenly sat upright, his eyes shooting fire. "You think it's me who decides? Yes, I'm the foreman and yes I speak for the men and women at the plant, but there's a committee of workers that decides and I'm not part of that committee."

"And why is that?" asked Carl.

"To make very clear to the management that I am not the workers' boss. I cannot tell them what to do. They tell me. That's how it is. And they don't give a hoot about your show, Pappas. The tide was high, that's what."

"There is nothing wrong with the workers' salaries and I've never heard of abuse," Grosmont said quickly before he could be interrupted.

"Yeah we're getting to that in a minute," said Carl.

"Nevertheless I'm tempted to walk away right now," said Grosmont. "Am I going to have to sit here and listen to all kinds of accusations of underpayment and workers' abuse that don't hold up in court?"

"First you answer my question," said the bizz jockey firmly. "How are you at diplomacy?"

"Not too good," yelled Bremen.

"When I joined the Desi Corporation, it was for expanding the business and finding new markets, developing new products. This is new territory. We have been putting the brakes on wages and all kinds of workers' benefits in order to stay competitive. We seem to have crossed some line, although we are still not competitive enough."

"Bullshit!" yelled Bremen.

"We need to take a step back, guys. Don't want to lose the

audience now, do we? Let's talk about the stuff you're manufacturing: the dry sachets."

Nine

In his airport hotel room, the fat man had fallen asleep on the bed, laptop on his huge belly, and was dreaming of the sales girl in the utilities shop. He had turned off the air conditioner because he didn't like the smell of it, but that had caused the room temperature to rise rapidly sending him off into a doze.

Fortunately he woke up within one hour. Even though he was annoyed at the loss of a precious hour that was meant for catching up with e-mail and other messages, he was relieved to find there was still time. What bothered him more than that, though, was the fact that the girl's voice was apparently haunting him. That hoarse sound... had he really heard her in his sleep? He didn't like these crushes on women who pass by too quickly. Most of the time he could erase them from his thoughts and his bloodstream as swift as they had arrived, simply by ignoring them for a while. He could fall in love with a stewardess on a two-hour flight and forget about her in approximately fifteen minutes after disembarking, providing he didn't take pictures on his cell phone.

But this time was different. He could still hear her hoarse voice in his ears and all kinds of unnerving thoughts popped up about her lips being so close to him. You never hear a hoarse voice from afar; they have to be close.

The fat man cursed and got up, went to the bathroom and turned on the shower. He ignored the oppressing heat in the room. He undressed himself and switched on a radio that was built into the bathroom wall, releasing a powerful radio voice that bounced on the tiles.

Man, you need to eat, he mumbled as he stepped into the cabin, raising his head to the steaming stream of water that showered down on him.

"First you answer my question," said the radio voice. "How are you at diplomacy?"

Ah, thought the fat man. The bizz jockey is attacking one of his guests again.

For a moment he was excited about this coincidence: he had stumbled upon his favorite radio show by accident.

Then there was a loud noise in the distance. The glass shower doors rumbled. He wasn't even sure what it was; the shower and the radio combined produced so many decibels that the new noise hardly reached him. It was gone immediately.

But there could be no mistake about the vibration that had come with the noise. It was tiny, but it was a vibration nonetheless. Something very heavy must have fallen and it must have happened nearby. Or was it an explosion?

The fat man turned off the water and opened the shower cabin door so clumsily that it was derailed, then stepped onto the floor in such a rush that he almost slipped. When he finally reached the door and jerked it open, he had lost whatever remained of his good mood —

He stared into a dark cloud of smoke, and the obvious beginning of a fire. He could see his bed burning.

My laptop! he shouted.

Then a sprinkler overhead was set off with a pang and water started to rain down on the burning bed and his open laptop. The scene was accompanied by the sound of an alarm, that mingled with the loud voices from the radio, blasting from the bathroom.

"There's this woman who mistook a dry sachet..." roared the radio voice.

Finally someone started banging on the door.

"Man!" the fat man said with a sigh. "Of all the lousy ways to spend an evening!"

By now he had forgotten all about the girl with the hoarse voice.

Ten

"Now that we're all familiar with the dry sachets, you gotta hear this," said Carl Pappas. "There's this woman who mistook a dry sachet for a..."

"Oh no!" said Jonathan Grosmont firmly. "I am not going to sit here and listen to you turn an honest product into something banal, Mr. Pappas."

Carl smiled. Through the window he saw Hitomi putting both arms up and slamming her left hand fist into her right hand palm, her face showing a reprimanding expression. She was not going to like the rest of the bizz jockey's joke about sachets.

"How many sachets does Desi ship annually?" said Pappas, quickly changing the topic.

"About half a billion," said Grosmont.

"And how many people quit their jobs annually?"

"I don't know," said Grosmont.

"But I do," said Bremen. "It's zero percent. All the people who work at the factory are locals and Desi is just too powerful a company in this area to pick a fight with. The local school master favors kids whose parents work at Desi."

"That's ridiculous," said Grosmont. "That's just gossip."

"In the past four years the amount of coffee breaks during work time has been reduced by forty percent and people who call in sick are required to visit the local doctor within one hour or they get fined. I can name a whole list of..."

"I'm sure you can," interrupted Carl. "I've seen the list. The Desi Corporation has developed a tough attitude to stay competitive. So be it. But is it worth this hassle, Jonathan? This strike, all the bad publicity... what if your decisions are a step too far? Have you considered that bashing your employees could be worse in the long run than being bashed by foreign competitors?"

"It's either that or move the plant to another location," said Grosmont. He sounded loud and clear.

"You haven't the guts," said Bremen, spitting out the word "guts" as if he was getting his teeth into an invisible enemy in font of him.

"Wait and see," hissed Grosmont from behind his teeth.

"Wait and see," repeated the bizz jockey.

Behind his window, Don Wozniak shoved some buttons on his console and suddenly the bizz jockey's voice became grand and full of echo.

"Don't miss out on the big spectacle, people. Get your camping gear and your fishing chair and line up outside the Desi factory fence. Bring a thermos flask full of coffee. Hell, bring your kids, because it's going to be a spectacle."

The echo was gone as fast as the sound engineer had created it.

"Very funny, Mr. Pappas," said Grosmont. "But if this man here is not going to be more diplomatic, it may come to just that."

"Just what?"

"A spectacle."

"Are you saying it's all my fault?" said Bremen.

"I am certainly not saying it isn't."

A chair fell.

"Well why don't you just step outside and put your fist where your mouth is, Mr. Gross," shouted Bremen.

"You mean put *your* fist where *my* mouth is."

"Yeah why don't you," laughed Pappas. "Why not fight the battle right here and right now, and get it over with."

"Sit down, Bremen," said Grosmont. "Before you lose the remains of your respectability as a foreman and union man."

Before his sentence was complete, his opponent was halfway across the studio table.

"I never had a talent for peacemaking," shouted Carl Pappas in the microphone, before he jerked off his earphones and leapt around the table.

From the other side of the glass, Don Wozniak looked on bemused, as Hitomi ran off, gesturing the WCBN Radio security officer in the room on the other side of the studio to move in with her.

"Be gentle, Sakamoto," he yelled after her. "They're just having a bit of fun. You know: F.U.N.?"

===

In the dark storage facility, the man with the scar had waited for a while till he was absolutely certain there was no other person around. Then he took out his cell phone and switched it on again. It had been off line ever since he had spoken to his client on the freight train; he couldn't risk being called in the midst of the operation of the past forty-eight hours. Moving around the factory in the dark, doing the work and remaining undetected was difficult enough as it is, with modern alarm systems and camera surveillance, and the noise of a cell phone ringtone was the last thing he needed. Even with the sound off, there was always the risk of its signal disturbing some surveillance equipment and raising suspicion. Even if it was a number he carried only for this particular client, he had still decided to switch it off. But now it was time to report that all was done and that he was experiencing an uncomfortable delay in his departure.

He had succeeded in placing the sachets and he had seen them take off in a large freight train. Because of the risk of explosions occurring on the train, he had decided to take the next train (or any other transport vehicle he could hide in) out of this place, but that had been a bad idea. All of a sudden, the very next morning, all the personnel here was going on strike and now there were people walking around twenty-four hours a day.

Plus his cell phone was dead.

The man touched the scar on the left side of his face. It had started to itch. He felt immensely inadequate; now his contact with the outside world was blocked by something as stupid as an empty battery. To begin with, he had chosen this particular model for its long battery life.

Suddenly there was a loud metal sound of a door on wheels being shoved open and fluorescent tubes jumped into action. The storage facility was flooded with light.

The man with the scar stood behind some crates and put the cell phone back in his coat. People were approaching rapidly.

"It's as if someone has been snooping around here these past days," a voice said.

A second voice responded immediately: "You and your suspicions. Got any proof to back it up before we start investigating? We're too busy for this."

"Check out this crate from nowhere," said the first voice.

The man with the scar peeked between a wall of crates and saw two uniformed men standing in the shade of another mountain of transport boxes. They were bent over something.

"It's not ours?"

"Nope."

"Must be from the transport company then."

"Listen, I've been doing rounds here for years, I would know. Anyway, there's a rule that there's nothing allowed here that's unknown to security. I have never seen a crate like this in the building. Look at it, it has a cooling unit inside. This is not your average run of the mill lunchbox you know."

"Well, it's empty now. Leave it here and we look into it later."

"It's completely without markings, so there won't be much to investigate. Aren't you worried about what was inside?"

"Mark it in the log," said the second voice. "I'm sure we'll find a perfectly logical explanation. Now I need you to come with me for more important stuff."

They walked away and soon the storage space was dark again.

The man with the scar sighed. He felt stuck between a crate

and a hard place. He had to get out of here.

Eleven

To white collar workers like Carl Pappas and Hitomi Sakamoto a factory had its own glamour. It was a place where people made their money more with their hands and brains, and less with their mouths, which made them heroes in the eyes of the bizz jockey and his producer. Both Carl and Hitomi had seen their share of smooth talkers and hollow howlers through the years, endless rows of people without any particular skills who had become rich and powerful nonetheless. Part of the success of The Boardroom was their quest for the other side of the coin. So they were always happy to meet the real workers of the world, people who pulled up their sleeves and got down to it without bragging about the end results. People like that could be found on Wall Street too, in the towers of Dubai, behind the glass facades of Shanghai and occasionally even in the City of London, but it was easier to go to a factory.

So there they were, sitting in a limousine approaching the Desi Corporation plant. There was a high fence with a closed gate, an enormous industrial complex behind it. It was difficult to see where it ended, this flat terrain covered with factories, sheds and auxiliary buildings, roads, silos and even its own railroad and cargo station.

Both before and beyond the gates were hundreds of people. They were hanging around, smoking under the billboard sign that showed the Desi Corporation logo and some advertising slogan, drinking coffee from thermos flasks, walking towards cars on large parking lots both inside and outside the gate, or into the large building right behind the gate, a building that housed both the janitor's quarters and the canteen.

"Wait," said Carl. "Can't we get out of the car right here? I want to talk to these folks."

"I sympathize with you, Sir," said the chauffeur, without turning his head, "but I've received specific instructions to escort you to the director's office."

"I'm sure Grosmont will quickly set you free on the premises, Carl," said Hitomi. "Anyway, they don't seem too pleased to see this car around here."

That was an understatement, as people started to yell things at the car and someone even hit it on the roof.

"Excuse the personnel," said the chauffeur coolly. "They're having problems of their own right now, you see."

There was more banging on the roof of the car.

"Stop this car," said Carl with all the authority he could muster. "I'm getting out right here to talk to these people."

"If you must," said the driver. "I trust you know what you are doing, Sir."

"You're a man of confidence," said Hitomi.

Outside the car, Carl Pappas faced something that could easily have turned into a mob — if he hadn't been the bizz jockey, a man with a certain feel for aggression that was about to surface.

"I'm Carl Pappas of The Boardroom," he yelled. "I'm here to look into your dispute and shed some light onto it on international radio."

"It's the bizz jockey!" a woman close to him yelled. "Three cheers for Carl Pappas!"

The crowd started to roar and Pappas was hoisted onto shoulders and carried through the gate, that swung open all of a sudden, and onto the factory grounds.

"Amazing," said the chauffeur to Hitomi. "I didn't know the man had such clout."

"He's a man of many talents," said the producer. "And defending the working class is one of them, and they know it."

The chauffeur maneuvered the car through the gate and the crowd, slowly. "You don't sound as if you are making a compliment, ma'am?"

"I do not always agree with him," said Sakamoto. "His views are radical sometimes, and there's always the danger of sudden escalation, you see. But don't worry, I like action any time of day."

Slowly the limousine drove out of the crowd and turned towards the only office building on the premises, and parked there.

Standing by the door was Jonathan Grosmont, accompanied by two heavily built men in dark suits wearing dark glasses and earphones wired to invisible devices inside their overcoats. Grosmont himself wore a light suit, but the expression on his face was considerably darker.

"Miss Sakamoto," he said, helping her out of the car. "I'm glad you made it here safely, but I still believe this whole mission is a mistake. The people here are extremely irritable right now. I may not have handled things too well on The Boardroom. And... where's Mr. Pappas?"

They stood there for a moment, Hitomi waiting patiently until Grosmont let go of her arm, which happened a wee bit beyond what was to be expected.

"Carl is amongst your workers," she said. "They'll deliver him to your doorstep in a moment, no doubt. But I disagree with what you say, I think you handled things exquisitely, Jonathan."

This softened the CEO's looks considerably. "Thank you. You're most kind. I wish more people felt like you."

"You've explained the international competitive position of the Desi Corporation quite clearly," said Hitomi. "In my opinion you must repeat your story as often as you can and through as many channels as you can. Keep hammering your point and, provided you are right, one day things will change."

"That'd better be soon," said Grosmont. His smile faded again, as he saw the plant's foreman, John Bremen, appear from the worker's crowd, along with the bizz jockey.

The two men approached in a relaxed fashion, while the cheering behind them faded.

"Shall we take a short tour of the complex?" said Grosmont. "It'll be my pleasure to show you around, as Mr. Bremen is obviously going to keep Mr. Pappas' mind occupied. I don't feel like competing with him any more than is strictly necessary."

They walked across the factory grounds, along the huge

buildings that were now quiet, the storage silos, full of desiccants, the hygroscopic substance that finds its way to users mostly in the form of gels. Close to the storehouse where the completed end products were stored, a long freight train stood still on its tracks. It seemed abandoned, its dozens of carriages stretching from the warehouse across an empty terrain of wild grass and low bushes towards the fence on the other side.

"Why don't they take the train away if there's no business here anyway?" said Hitomi."

"The men have closed the gate across the tracks and sent the train personnel away," said Grosmont. "A slight overkill if you ask me. Now we're not only losing money everyday because there are no sales, but we're also going to receive a claim from the logistics company."

"They may go on strike too," sounded Bremen's loud voce.

He appeared from around a corner, followed by Carl Pappas.

"You don't say," said Grosmont. "Is that an option?"

"Yes, so I've heard."

"Yeah," said Carl in his typical casual way, "the Desi strike seems to have hit a chord among the nation's workers. It may spread."

"Just like the bird flu," said Grosmont.

"The bird flu kills people," said Bremen. "This is about improving the lives of hard working people and their families, about their kids' education..."

"And about their kids being all out of work because their parents bankrupted another fine company!"

"OK guys, that'll do," said Pappas. "We're here to talk about this with open minds. You didn't do too well on live radio, so we're looking for a chance to give this a reboot. In the end you're going to have to come together." He looked at the two adversaries, from one to the other, and back. "You know, come together?" He sang the last two words, a famous melody that made both Grosmont and Bremen relax a bit.

"You're crazy," said Grosmont, shaking his head to the bizz jockey. "But you're all right. Let's go inside and I'll get all of you some coffee. Mrs. Sakamoto, may I?" He offered the producer his arm.

She took it and they walked back to the office.

"Charming, don't you think?" said Carl to Bremen.

"Dangerous," Bremen corrected him. "Don't mistake a predator for a charmer. While you think he's being courteous, he could be buying your producer away from your show. Thát is the kind of man he is."

They followed Sakamoto and Grosmont.

"He's just being tough for the owner's sake, I guess," said Carl. "As soon as they can accuse him of being a wussy, he's a goner."

Bremen laughed and hit the bizz jockey on his shoulder. "One thing he's right about though," he said. "You're all right."

Twelve

From under his Fedora, Lieutenant Carlsberg looked at the black spot inside the city's central library. He touched his mustache. His brown raincoat was giving off steam from the cold outside, and his Rolex still felt like a wristband made of ice. At least he was inside now.

"Not funny at all," he said to the fire chief, who recognized him and shook his hand from behind the red white crime scene ribbon.

"Goes without saying," said the fire chief.

"Well, you didn't hear it from me then," replied Carlsberg.

The two men had known each other for years and had developed a couple of greeting routines, and this was one of them.

A lady from the library staff brought coffee. Carlsberg took it with him as he dived under the ribbon to where the fire chief was standing.

"Four heavily wounded, one dead," said the police officer on duty who was standing close to the black area, holding a tablet. "They've already been taken away. As it turns out, a bag fell from the table to the floor and then blew up. Or at least that's a witness version. Anyway, the table shielded many people from the blow. It could have been worse."

"Thank you officer," said Carlsberg. For a moment he considered reprimanding his young colleague for offering an unwanted opinion. Who cares if things could have been a lot worse, if they could just as easily have been a lot better? Crime is bad to begin with, Carlsberg felt, so things can basically never be worse. They can only be better. But he decided to let it go and focused instead on the damage done.

"Any traces of the explosive or of the package it was in?" he asked, testing the coffee with his lips. It was hot enough to speed up global warming.

"Actually yes, it's over there," said the police officer and he pointed to a table where small plastic bags laid, containing evidence.

Carlsberg walked to the man who was bent over the table.

"Hi Joe," he said. "What's that?"

The man turned his head, looking up at Carlsberg. "A backpack," he said. "Nothing special."

Joe Portland was one of the police department's forensics experts and usually among the first people to arrive on a crime scene. Actually he was considered a bit of a creep for showing up so fast that it sometimes looked conspicuous. He was a tall, boney man, everything protruding from his body that could possibly protrude, as if all these body parts were competing with his Adam's apple, a rock-like formation that seemed to be floating in front of his throat.

"There's always something special," said Carlsberg.

"You name it," said Portland, stubborn.

"Was it an old bag?"

For a moment, Portland was silent. Then he said: "Who cares?"

"Well, was it?"

"Actually, it was brand-new," said Portland. He rolled his eyes, which had a dizzying effect on the spectator. Portland had bulging eyes and any movement they made was a big deal to begin with. It was never clear if he was bored with the details of forensics or that he was just always in a hurry to get the job done and move on to the next one.

"Funny," said Carlsberg. "That's the second backpack that's exploded in forty-eight hours. There was one on the airport."

"I know," said Portland. "The one in the hotel room. Guy was in the shower, so he was lucky. It was also a new bag, in case you're interested."

The huge, bulging eyes stared at Carlsberg like if they had a mouth they would love to eat him. Red veins pulsated.

"How do you know that?"

"I checked the file this morning. I check all files of all my forensic colleagues in the larger area. Wanna see?"

The thin, boney man presented a tablet and logged in to a website with such agility, that he scared the lieutenant once again.

Does everything this man does have to freak me out? Carlsberg thought. Then he looked at the screen. There were images of the remains of a burned backpack, and the interior of a hotel room.

"What ya thinking boss?" said Portland. "Talk to me. I can help but I'm in a hurry to get to another job."

"Two new bags," said Carlsberg. "If it were three, I'd say it couldn't have been a coincidence."

"Someone blowing up brand new backpacks for fun, you think?"

"No, forget it," said Carlsberg. "It's probably nothing."

The boney man grabbed his sleeve. "No wait," he said, suddenly panting. "What if you're on to something." The large eyes got even wider. "A grand scheme?"

"Unlikely. That happens only in movies."

"No. Think logical. What do all brand new bags have in common?" said Portland.

"They smell weird," said Carlsberg.

"Well, yes, I guess they do. Listen, I'll pick up a brand new bag and if I think of anything I'll give you a holler, how's that?"

The lieutenant smiled. "That's fine with me, Portland. Just make sure it's a bag you can use, OK? Don't just throw money away."

===

Fifteen minutes later, still talking to the library staff about the explosion and just about to start a review of the surveillance tapes, Carlsberg's cell phone rang.

"Carlsberg."

"Dry sachets," said Portland on the other end.

"Excuse me?"

"New bags or backpacks or any type of bag that come from the factory and are designed for carrying laptops or that sort of delicate equipment around," said Portland, talking in a high-pitched voice and stumbling over his words, "have basically only one thing in common: they contain dry sachets.

You know, those little bags of silicon drops that suck up moisture? They all have 'em."

"Come on Portland, get a life."

"No, really. I found one myself in a bag that I had owned for years. They're tucked way down deep into the bags, so you may fail to notice them."

Carlsberg was walking towards the security officer's desk to check out some surveillance tapes. "I don't have time for this, Portland. What do these sachets have to do with this? Exploding sachets? Is that what you are saying?"

"Why not? Put them into new bags in a warehouse somewhere, they spread across the world nicely. These sachets are supposed to be there, so no one will think anything of it."

"I gotta go now," said Carlsberg, raising his hand to gesture "hello" to the security officer. "Just one thing: have you found anything to back this up?"

"Well, some typical stuff, explosive residues. It was a small dosage. But no silicon residue, if that's what you mean."

"No silicons, huh. OK. If a third case pops up, a third brand new bag exploding, I'll rethink your theory, Portland."

He ended the conversation and put the phone away. Portland had just confused him more instead of less, with these big eyes of his.

Man, these eyes were huge.

===

The fat man was sweating.

"This is the umpteenth time I'm talking to the police," he

complained. "I'm two days behind schedule now and still I'm being delayed. Can't we keep this short? I'm really tired and I need to get to work."

"My colleagues tell me you haven't been all too cooperative during the investigation," said Carlsberg. "Perhaps if you just told them what they need to know, they could go home sooner."

They were sitting in the hotel lobby, a security officer standing next to them. The fat man looked at a mayonnaise stain on his shirt, nervous under the lieutenant's stare.

"Sure," he said. "Go ahead, accuse me. What did I do? If I hadn't been in the shower, I would have been dead, they told me."

"What was on the laptop?"

"Oh, that again. Everybody's asking me about my laptop. It's gone. It's damaged beyond repair. It doesn't matter what I say was on it, because I can't prove nothing."

Carlsberg kept on staring. "They say you have been up- and downloading massive amounts of data while you were in your room and that you refuse to explain what it was. Just show them what it was and they're off your back."

Finally, the fat man found his strength again. "What if I'm embarrassed to say it was porn? What if it's industrial secrets? What if I'm working for Beijing or Moscow or some secret service. What if I was just streaming movies? As long as there's no real reason I'm not going to show nothing to no one. And what if it was someone in the next room?"

"They know it was you and they know you transferred massive amounts of data through encrypted channels. You're using pathways that make you look suspicious, that's all.

Listen, I'm not investigating you, so perhaps you'll take a friendly advice from me?"

"I'll see."

"These secret service guys," said Carlsberg, "they figure if someone is moving across secret roads on the internet, he's got something to hide. They're going to harass you indefinitely, even after this case is closed."

"My lawyer is going to make sure they're not," the fat man said, stubbornly. "The evidence is destroyed anyway, so it's a case on hold. Anything else? Why don't you guys look for whoever tried to blow me up?"

"You got me there," said Carlsberg. "That's exactly what I'm doing. You said to the officer that your bag was brand new. You purchased it on the airport, you say. Did you remove a dry sachet from it after you bought it, by any chance?"

"A whát?"

The lieutenant stood up. "Thank you, Sir. That'll be all."

The fat man watched him go, perplexed, unable grasp the point of the conversation he had just been a part of.

Carlsberg walked straight out of the hotel, as puzzled as the man he left behind. The dry sachets didn't leave him alone. In the back of his mind, there was a significance to it, as if these small items had been waiting for him to discover their secret purpose in life.

Thirteen

During the intermission, Philemon Solo went to the foyer of the theater to catch his breath again. The first half of *Macbeth* had exhausted him. It was one thing to go to a Shakespeare play hoping to learn about politics and scheming and how to rise to power, it was another thing to confront a theatrical experiment. Because that's what this show was: there were no props, the actors all wore the same black clothes and moved around as little as possible. There was no visual spectacle.

But Solo, WCBN Radio's managing director and boss of the bizz jockey, liked to put himself to the test, so when Hitomi Sakamoto had suggested that seeing the new *Macbeth* would be too much for him to digest, he'd risen to the occasion.

A bit too hastily, he had to admit, and now all one could do was relax the nerves with a glass of wine. He was going to sit through the whole thing because Sakamoto, that iron Japanese producer, was going to humiliate him in public if he didn't — and she'd know even without being here.

With his thoughts too full of the play and its myriad meanings, Solo bumped into a woman — or she bumped into him, that's always difficult to tell when you're in a crowd.

"Pardon me."

They both said this, simultaneously.

This had never happened to Phil Solo. Never before. People said things like "Excuse me" and "Sorry", but never "Pardon".

Solo spread his hands and gently grabbed the lady's upper arms. "Did I hurt you?"

"After all that verbal violence, I can take it," the woman said.

If she was an ageing woman well into her twilight years, she was also an ageing beauty. There was no doubt about that: here was a woman who had to have been a starlet or a model in her younger years. Her face was now older, there were plenty of wrinkles, but she was still beautiful and her appearance was that of royalty: she wore a red robe, all the way down to the floor, with a necklace of white pearls, a large, waving curl of hair way down to her shoulders and white teeth, as straight as a movie star's.

The both of them stood out in the crowd that swirled around them, for they were tall people.

"Nevertheless," said Phil with a bombast that would have suited the Macbeth actor in the play, "I am going to get whatever it is you were going to drink or eat. Please allow me to redeem myself in this way."

"Most kind," said the woman. "I am Catherine."

It was unavoidable. By seeing the play, Philemon Solo had become a wee bit too theatrical and as a result he kissed the lady's hand on a whim. But perhaps a Shakespeare play has this effect on all people, for she allowed him this gesture, and smiled.

"I am Philemon," said Solo. "Please wait here and all will be well." He disappeared into the crowd.

A man in a dark suit, almost half a century younger than the lady, whispered to her. "Should I discourage him, ma'am?"

"Absolutely not," she replied, her voice so low that none of the people around them would be able to understand anything she said. "Don't you recognize a gentleman when you see one? Just stand back and remain in the background."

===

On live radio, bizz jockey Carl Pappas was steaming ahead through the items on his business talk show The Boardroom, and he was eager to score.

"I've looked at the numbers of your company, Selig," he said to a voice on the phone. "You people have had twenty-five years of growth. And now you are dealing with two years of stalling sales — not even dropping, only stalling — and everybody's getting depressed. That's sick."

"That's how the economy works, Carl," said Selig, an older voice with the effects of nicotine and whiskey embedded within it. "If there's no growth, there's nothing."

"You should emphasize the importance of a pause in your company's success," said Pappas. "Go on CNN. Talk to Richard Quest. Make sure shareholders understand that after so much growth you need to take a break from expansion and reconsider your position. Reconsider your future. Any business that never stops, runs out of steam sooner or later. Defy the general opinion, defy the growth mantra."

"People will not relax until we've proven the current

slowdown is only temporary," said the older voice.

"I disagree," said the bizz jockey. "You need to speak about plans and the future and so forth. Be realistic. Realism is like an elixir for the stock exchange. Bye Selig."

Behind one of the studio windows, sound engineer Don Wozniak hit a tune that told the regular listeners: this call has ended.

"And after the break I need to talk to all of you people about dry sachets," said Carl. "You know, those tiny bags that keep your vitamin bottles and your computer bags dry. I went to the plant of the Desi Corporation where they're on strike and talked to all involved and I have a couple of nuts to crack about that."

During the break, Hitomi Sakamoto walked into the studio room where Carl Pappas was looking through his papers, preparing himself for the item after the commercial break. She handed him his cell phone.

"It's that policeman, Carlsberg."

"Is that really necessary? I have two minutes."

"Carl Evangelos Pappas, I know precisely how many minutes you have."

He took the phone. "Carlsberg, don't tell me you've arrested my boss," he said.

"I've said it before: you're not as funny as you are on radio, Pappas," said Carlsberg. "I need to talk to you about dry sachets."

"Let's do it fast before I become thirsty."

===

Under an enlarged photo portrait of Marlon Brando, Catherine Gretta and Phil Solo sipped their glasses of red wine. The age difference between them was at least a third of a century, but neither of them cared.

"I was indeed a model when I was very young," said Catherine. "Also my parents were wealthy. This combination of beauty and influence meant that I never was a starlet in the literal sense; I never had to sleep with a Hollywood producer to open doors. My parents did that for me. Not the sleeping, mind you."

"So why didn't you pursue a career in modeling or movies?" said Phil.

"I felt hollow," the woman said. "Of course this was slumbering inside me. But it wasn't until I met my late husband that a longing for another life was woken up. By the time we got married, I had retreated to a life of building business and charity work. For most of my life I have evaded the limelight."

"And quite successfully so," said Phil. "Although I have heard of you, of course. You are the majority owner and chairperson of the Desi Corporation."

"Well, well. Other than good looking, you are also well informed. You don't come across such a combination often these days."

"And many other corporations, for that matter."

"Phil — may I call you Phil? — you really need to change topics. We are on a cultural night out in the town and talking about my slumbering interests in the corporations my husband has left me is not necessarily... Let's say I am sure you have many other qualities other than business."

"I will leave that up to you to decide, Mrs. Gretta."

"Catherine, if you please."

"Catherine."

"I will watch your every move with great scrutiny and let you know. So tell me, you run WCBN Radio?"

"In fact, I do. There's a board of course, but they're in the background. My primary concern is making sure that the Bizz Jockey doesn't go too far on The Boardroom."

The gong, announcing the second half of the play, roared through his voice. Catherine put her glass down on the small, high table next to them. She then took Phil's glass right out of his hands and put it down as well.

"You're coming with me," she said. "I have a box and we haven't finished talking yet."

===

Right in front of Carl Pappas, one of the laptop screens was counting down the last thirty seconds before The Boardroom went live again. The digits filled the screen.

"I'd say it's just a coincidence," said the bizz jockey. "I'm not taking any of this serious."

"Neither am I. But if I'm right, a third explosion will occur real soon and when it does, I'll be getting back to you. OK?"

"Sure. Bye."

Then it was 2-1-0 and the "Live" sign switched on.

===

As *Macbeth* was rapidly seeing his world unraveling on the stage, Phil Solo was whispering in Catherine Gretta's ear like a gentleman, emphasizing her everlasting beauty in a world where real women were becoming a scarcity, an endangered species embedded by artificial women in the media, silicones and surgical proceedings and vitamins and liposuctions. He wasn't even posturing. The WCBN Radio boss was very good at posturing, but he was sincere this time, being overwhelmed by this woman from another time, from another class. She had a face that suited her age, without the strange widened eyes and bulging lips and cheeks that were so often seen, the trails of surgeons' knives.

During the moments when they were both silent, he felt his confusion. As a single man he was used to attention from all kinds of women, the young interns who looked up to him as to a man of power and wealth, the account managers and secretaries, who regarded him as someone who was doing better than their own partners, the elder women who were impressed but of no interest to him. The only woman he knew who remained outside of his grasp was of course Hitomi Sakamoto, but he felt that was a good thing: he needed a strong producer who could handle the bizz jockey and charm important guests at the same time.

And then, just as he was getting comfortable, Catherine Gretta whispered in his ear: "We will have to speak about your bizz jockey attacking my dry sachets company though. That strike is costing me millions and you people are only making it worse. I've heard those broadcasts."

On stage someone said: "We shall not spend a large expense of time."

Seeing Phil Solo's face aghast, Catherine whispered: "Oh, don't worry, Phil. We can work it out."

===

The taxi driver took the computer bag and the suitcase from the business man and put them in the trunk of his black Mercedes. His car was of the luxurious kind, driven only for special clients. The driver opened the rear door close to the pavement in front of the hotel and let the businessman in. They were look-alikes, in a way: both in their fifties, their hair semi-long in a gray curl, clean-shaven, a square chin and radiating blue eyes, and their clothes clean and dark-blue. Of course one was a uniform and the other a suit, but they made a nice couple.

Of course they weren't, for they didn't speak, they didn't know each other and they didn't care. They just got into the same car and drove off through the night city.

When the bag in the trunk exploded, and then the car's gas tank and then the entire car, these men went as they came: silent, and unfamiliar.

Fourteen

Hitomi Sakamoto didn't like men who talked too loud in public. As a matter of fact, she didn't like men who talked too soft either. Men were supposed to talk at exactly the right volume and keep the barking for combat and the whispering for their woman.

So spending an hour in the *Gulag* was kind of torture to her: there was hardly a man around who talked at a volume she was comfortable with.

There was Lieutenant Carlsberg, who had a monotonous way of speaking that tended to become too loud when someone contradicted or interrupted him. There was the CEO of the Desi Corporation, Jonathan Grosmont, who kept on speaking in a soft way that was irritating; she suspected him of lowering his voice to get more focus and attention from the people around him. And there was her boss, the bizz jockey, but he was all right. Carl Pappas was one of the very few men who had a perfect voice: low, authoritative, decisive and, if necessary, very loud. She had once had the audacity to ask Pappas' girlfriend at a party if he had ever whispered in a romantic way and she had confirmed this.

"It's rare, but it happens with Carl," the beautiful woman had said.

Hitomi had persuaded Jonathan Grosmont with her usual charm and escorted him here for a meeting with Pappas and Carlsberg, without telling him what it was all about.

"You are such an interesting man," said Hitomi. "Please don't leave immediately after the meeting, we must have lunch so we can talk some more."

She could be such a liar.

Jonathan Grosmont appeared unimpressed. "Surely you're making a joke?" he said loud. "The stuff we make is not an explosive and the factory is waterproof. If you're accusing the Desi Corporation of distributing explosive dry sachets, you are going to face a lawyers' squad the size of an army."

"We're not accusing you of anything, Jonathan," said Carl. "WCBN Radio has its own army of lawyers. I wouldn't dream of such a thing."

"You are not going to say this on the radio then?"

"No," said Carl.

"We need your help," said Carlsberg. "Before I do anything, I want to hear your opinion. Last night I got confirmation that there's been a third explosion that involves a brand new computer bag. Normally I wouldn't look into this sort of thing, it's too outrageous. But the lack of congruity is exactly what makes it all congruent: these are random explosions, located roughly at the same distance from the factory. It could be, that whoever is doing this, is planting explosive sachets inside your factory."

"Some of these sachets go into products that stay shelved

for years," said Grosmont.

"I have nothing else to go on," said Carlsberg. "I must look into this. Yesterday afternoon I expected the next one to go off within hours. It was just a hunch, but there you are: the taxi exploded close to midnight. I simply cannot ignore it."

From the face of the Desi CEO came a winter front. It was cold as ice.

"I think it would be good to emphasize something," said Hitomi, mingling in the conversation for the first time. She had merely been taking notes and ordering coffee. All heads turned towards here. "I think Jonathan is not looking forward to the prospect of the Desi factory being searched by a large police force."

Fortunately, Carlsberg jumped at the opportunity to ease the tension. "Obviously not," he said. "But you can count on public unrest as soon as any of this gets out and people discover that we're all unable to do anything about it. The very least we can do is take random samples from the shipments the bags originated from. See what we find."

Jonathan Grosmont looked out the window. "This really is all coming down at the same time," he sighed. "Most unfortunate."

Then he jerked his head back to his companions at the table. "Of course, I will cooperate. I'll ask our internal security chief to get those samples."

"I know when and where the exploding bags were sold," said Carlsberg. "That should be easy. But you should move carefully; if there are more sachets filled with explosive it could be very dangerous. Please make sure your man calls me before he does anything at all so I can involve our bomb disposal guy."

The proprietor of the *Gulag*, Mrs. Yekaterina, known as Katie to her regular guests, appeared at the table out of thin air. She smiled at Hitomi and then eyed the bizz jockey.

"Serious business today, Carl? Can we expect an explosive radio show tonight?"

"Katie, my beautiful lady of the night," Pappas said aloud. "It's you. Whenever I'm close to you, things suddenly seem to matter."

"My dear bizz jockey." The middle-aged woman, always at ease, stood in the restaurant as if it were the center of the earth, her arms akimbo. Her bleached hair added to her stature and her whitened teeth instilled a cocktail of warmth and fear in the men she smiled at. "I want you to relax. Why so serious? It cannot have anything to do with me. If it were up to me, we were all dancing on the table and drinking vodka."

She winked at Hitomi, who didn't like being part of Katie's banter at all.

"It must be the coffee," Katie said, walking off. "But I'll get all of you some more nonetheless."

"That's a start," said Carl. "Now, we need to do something else. We need to find out why someone wants to put the Desi Corporation in such a position."

"There are other companies making dry sachets," said Grosmont.

"None of them as huge as you," said Hitomi, touching the man's sleeve.

She's such a smooth operator, thought Carl.

"Does anybody hold a grudge against your company?" said

Carlsberg.

"No. None other than the workers," said Grosmont. "They want more money. But hey, that's no reason to throw explosives around, I guess."

"And what about the owner? Does the owner have something to fear?" said Carl.

"Not that I know of," said Carlsberg. "Listen, there's really nothing more I can tell you. I must be on my way, there's urgent business for me." His gestures suggested he was about to stand up and leave.

"I'd like to talk to the owner," said Pappas. "Can we talk to him?"

"Yes," Carlsberg agreed. "Good idea." He stroke his moustache.

"Her," said Grosmont. "But I'm sorry, there is no way I can get you in touch with Mrs. Gretta."

"Excuse me? You're the CEO. You talk to her daily," said Carl, raising his voice.

"Take it easy, big fella," said Katie, who appeared again to bring new coffee.

"I don't talk to her daily and I cannot put you in touch with her. She stays in the background as much as she can. She doesn't like to be seen in public for some reason. She was once a member of the rich and famous, you know, movie stars and rock stars and media moguls. But she withdrew and won't have any of it. She only shows up as chairperson of the board once or twice a year, that's about it. She reads all memoranda on all of her companies though, but her affairs are handled through other people."

"Sure," said Carl. "But you are going to introduce us to her nonetheless. You have the authority. And if you don't, Mr. Policeman here has all the authority you need."

"I doubt that," said Grosmont. "Try to get close to her, she's hiding behind a small army of lawyers. But you have to understand: I simply cannot do it."

"Explain," said Pappas.

"The man who was CEO before me, was fired and sued because he drove up to her house and rang her doorbell unannounced. She was still furious three years later."

They were silent for a moment, looking at Grosmont perplexed.

Katie, who had just finished pouring coffee, said: "Well, there's your woman with balls."

Fifteen

We all have a part to play on the grand stage of life. There's not much you can do about that. Fortunately, some of us get to trade places every now and then. This time, the bizz jockey Carl Pappas and his boss, Philemon Solo, had done just that. It was a reversal of the natural order at WCBN Radio.

The dreamy bizz jockey had somehow pulled his head out of the clouds of business utopia and sat at his desk on the seventeenth floor of the WCBN Radio building, contemplating the very practical facts of the dry sachets explosions, the strike at the Desi plant and the distant owner, Mrs. Catherine Gretta.

On the other hand, his boss Philemon Solo had left his practical, logical and calculating self behind him end had entered a state of bliss. Now, he was the dreamer. For once, Philemon Solo didn't worry about all that could be done wrong by the bizz jockey this morning, all the legal problems he would be facing or all the money he was going to have to cough up. He thought of *Macbeth*. That much was obvious when he started speaking to Carl.

"I saw Lady Macbeth last night. Astonishing."

Behind his desk, Pappas looked up from his laptop screen. "It's *Macbeth*, Phil. Lady Macbeth is just a character. It's *Macbeth*."

"I know that," said Solo. "But does it really matter? It's the thought that counts."

On any other day Carl would have noticed the incoherence of his boss's remarks, but now he just looked back at his screen. "There's something going on and it's one of those things where you know the solution is too stupid for words. It's right under my nose but I can't see it."

"I don't have that problem," said Solo. "There's nothing wrong with my eyes. Amazing how age can sometimes... be an improvement."

Carl looked up, puzzled. "What áre you talking about?" He slammed his laptop shut. "Listen Phil, I'm in a cul-de-sac here. You know how I hate that. Don't you? I could fill four shows with this topic if I crack it, I'm really on to something but we're stuck." He leaned back towards the window, raised both arms to the ceiling. "I have no idea what to do next."

Solo plunged himself in one of the chairs opposite Carl's Desk.

It was a long standing tradition that Philemon Solo mingled in all Carl's affairs, offered him opinions and criticism at all times. But it was highly unusual for Carl to ask his boss to assist on editorial matters. He could order a whole team around anytime, trainees, reporters, editors and so forth; Solo just made sure they could all do their jobs at full steam.

"I met a woman last night at the theater that you are not going to believe," said Phil, in an unexpected and quite unusual candid moment. "She's the owner of several businesses, acting as a semi-retired chairperson. Or should I say chair lady? She's the toughest, strongest mature woman I have spoken to in years — your Miss Sakamoto excepted — and I'm sure they call her the Iron Lady behind her back."

Carl stood up and looked out the window. "Good for you, Phil. Good for you." A passenger plane hovered low over the office buildings, towards the airport at the city's edge in the distance. Only a fraction of its engine's roar penetrated the window, but it took Pappas away from his meandering thoughts. He looked back and said: "Say no more, Phil. How long will it last this time? You and the ladies? It's the same old song and you expect me to be thrilled every time it happens. Will you never grow up?"

The boss jumped up from the chair and started walking through the room without a purpose, passing the desk, the windows, a cabinet with awards, another cabinet with files and a laptop on top of it. "Just wait until you meet Catherine Gretta, Mr. Bizz Jockey Carl Pappas. You will take back those words and hand me over your girlfriend. You're such a liar; I never expect you to be thrilled and I hardly ever tell you anything about women. What do you mean: I and the ladies? I..."

"Did you just say Gretta as in Mrs. Catherine Gretta?" Carl shouted as he ran quickly towards Solo.

The noise was enough to startle Phil Solo. He stopped pacing and looked at Pappas, like a man who just made up his mind. "Forget it, Carl. I'm talking to the wrong man here." He wanted to turn around and walk away, but the bizz jockey grabbed his arm.

"I can't believe it!" yelled Carl.

From the doorway, the voice of producer Hitomi Sakamoto came loud and clear: "What's that? Phil, you actually followed my advice and went to see *Macbeth*?"

Both men looked at her, confused, not knowing whether to be annoyed by the interruption or not. It was the bizz jockey who got hold of the situation first.

"You hold that thought, Hitomi," he said, with a powerful voice and his index finger raised at the producer. At the same time he looked Phil Solo straight in the eye and said: "If you are dating Catherine Gretta, you are going to introduce me to her *right now*."

In the doorway, Hitomi Sakamoto put both arms akimbo and opened her mouth.

But this time it was Phil Solo who raised his finger to silence her. "Don't say it, Sakamoto. Not now."

But the producer had already decided that this was a wrong moment for anything and walked away through the corridor, while behind her two voices were raised to uncomfortable levels.

===

John Bremen, the factory foreman and leader of the Desi factory workers' strike, never grew tired of arguing and talking and pep talking. So that was not the reason he had decided to take a break and get some fresh air. He left behind the hundreds of men and women hanging around the front entrance and the restaurant, drinking gallons of coffee and smoking too much, saying he had to visit the toilet. He walked right into the workers' restaurant building and walked straight out of it on the other side. Just to make sure he could take a walk alone and think straight. Because that was the real reason he needed a few moments alone: to think things over. In all the turmoil one needed to clear the head every now and then and contemplate. There was always the risk of overlooking the obvious and this risk was especially big when you were in a crowd. Crowds don't do a lot of thinking.

So John Bremen walked across the factory grounds, passed by some buildings and tried not to stumble over anything because there were only a few lanterns shedding light on the concrete. He knew a strike of this size was going to make a turn for the better or the worse very soon. With hundreds of families involved, national media starting to take interest in the case and the company making huge losses, there was not much time. It was going to be a court case with the risk of violence and failure for both parties, or it was going to be a quick wrap. All he needed was a long, long meeting with the board of directors, with a lot of shouting going on outside the boardroom, a meeting that went on into the wee small hours of the morning. That was his biggest chance of success: wearing them out and then striking a deal.

So he went through several scenarios in his head, while he turned another corner of the factory building. He was walking alongside the freight train, a large, long hulk of a shadow in the moonlight. This shipping area had large floodlights, but they were all switched off.

Right in the middle of a third scenario in his head — a proposal to close the two foreign Desi factories and bring all those jobs back to this location, in return for a freeze of workers' salaries — John Bremen heard a noise. It was a soft clunking, as if someone was opening a wagon door. He stood still immediately, and while he did that, one of his shoes made a squeaking sound on the concrete.

Then it was silent again. Bremen turned his head in an attempt to pick up sounds from several directions, but he heard nothing. Then he sank through his knees, bent over and looked under the train towards the other side, to see if there was anything there. All he saw was the concrete terrain, pale in the vague light of the moon.

Perhaps it had been a bird pecking away at the steel of the train, mistaking it for wood, he thought. Woodpeckers had to be stupid.

He got up again, but before he had straightened his back entirely he felt a sharp pain on the back of his head, and what little light remained that night flooded out of view.

Sixteen

The mansion stood on a hill, surrounded by a lush garden of lawns and rhododendron perimeters, several small outbuildings, a tennis court, a swimming pool, a small forest and a brick wall that was covered with ivy. When Phil Solo announced himself through the intercom below the lion's statue at the entrance, the wrought iron gate swung open. He looked at Pappas with a smile on his face, to see if the bizz jockey was impressed.

But large houses didn't make a dent in Carl Pappas' consciousness. He had long ago decided that having an opinion about the size of one's home was a waste of time. In his long years as a business talk radio host he had learned that riches could come to anybody; you don't have to be particularly clever or good to own a large mansion. Some are inherited, some are stolen, and some have been properly worked for. You can't tell by looking at the outside.

Never mistake a huge house for an angel's halo.

"Nice," said Carl, because he did appreciate the architecture. He saw influences of Art Deco and the organic architecture of Frank Lloyd Wright. The stained glass windows by the front door reached three stories high and poured their cheerful light over the visitors as they approached the main building.

They were standing in the library of the mansion when a large door was opened by a servant and Catherine Gretta marched in. In spite of her considerable age she walked briskly and stood in front of Philemon Solo before either of them had been able to say anything.

"How absolutely delightful to see you again so soon, my dear," she said as she kissed Solo on both cheeks.

Carl could tell they were not air kisses. The lips were touching cheeks carefully. They took their time chatting away, most of it right outside of the bizz jockey's earshot.

At some point Pappas had had enough. "Funny how the two of you are on speaking terms," he said, "in spite of everything that's going on at the Desi Corporation."

Solo and Mrs. Gretta were holding each other by the elbows and looked at Carl simultaneously.

Then Mrs. Gretta took a step back and confronted her other guest. "Philemon here is not responsible for the editorial stance of WCBN Radio concerning my business interests," she said and she sounded as cold as ice. Then she pointed a finger at him. "But yóu are."

"I am just a channel, Mrs. Gretta. I've given as much airtime to your disgruntled factory workers as to your CEO, Mr. Grosmont. It's up to them, I don't really have an opinion about the strike."

"Oh but you dó, Mr. Pappas."

"Are we all on a first name base here or am I excluded from

the pleasantries?" said Carl.

Mrs. Gretta walked towards him until she was too close for comfort. "You are excluded, Mr. Pappas. Philemon insisted I see you, otherwise you wouldn't be here. But I do believe you are giving to much airtime to the strike at Desi. With all that publicity, people get overheated all too easily"

A door opened and a young woman wearing an apron came in.

"But let's not forget our manners," said Mrs. Gretta. "You're here now, so let me make you feel welcome nonetheless. If we are going to argue, we need the caffeine, don't you agree?"

They nodded, coffees of various degrees of sophistication were ordered, and then they sat down.

"I don't like your style, Mr. Pappas," said Mrs. Gretta. "You presume to reside in a kind of self made court, where business people are facing their verdict."

"Thank you, ma'am," said Carl. "I'm honored to have you among my audience."

"Don't flatter yourself, bizz jockey," she snapped. "I haven't listened to you in years. Only now... I'm forced to stay tuned."

The young servant brought in the coffee on a tray on wheels.

"I'm sorry you feel that way," said Carl. "I will spare you the embarrassment of me defending my radio show. If ever you feel like you want to tell me why you dislike my style on live radio, in front of ten million listeners, you are welcome."

The old lady laughed out loud and took her time laughing. Her amusement was so convincing that after a while Solo and

Pappas joined in. Even the young servant couldn't suppress a grin as she walked away, eyeing the bizz jockey thoroughly on her way out.

"I must hand it to you, Mr. Pappas, you are a funny man. I can see how you keep ten million listeners in your pocket. Well, good for you. But no doubt you've heard enough about me to know that I am on the verge of becoming a total recluse. I have no need to hear my name mentioned on the biggest international talk radio show around. I want my privacy."

The laughter had ended. They all took their coffee and drank a bit.

"And if you are here to put in a good word for these strikers on the Desi plant, you are mistaken. I will not bow to their demands."

"Isn't that up to your board of directors, Mrs. Gretta," said Carl.

"If they haven't the guts, I will be the last man standing, Mr. Pappas," said Mrs. Gretta. "My husband's business hasn't survived for half a century to be brought down by weaklings. And by weaklings, and you may quote me on that at least, I mean both management and workers. International competition is not for the weak hearted. It is for soldiers. So instead of all the chitchat you're doing on your show, you should be asking these people if they're up to it. Are they really the soldiers that are going to win the economic wars?"

The men were wise enough to refrain from commenting. This was especially hard for Pappas, who liked hard talk about economic wars.

So, ignoring her point, Carl said: "Mrs. Gretta, we are here for an entirely different matter, and one that no doubt matters to you. I must ask you if there is anyone in particular who dislikes you or the Desi Corporation enough to execute a terrorist attack."

Once again they all sat there in silence.

Carl thought Phil Solo was unusually quiet.

Phil Solo thought coming here might have been a bad idea.

"Go ahead, Mr. Pappas," said Mrs. Gretta.

"The police have reason to believe that some dry sachets from the Desi Corporation are stacked with explosives. They are being exported from the factory and a couple have exploded in a hundred kilometer range so far. If this is so, things may get worse very soon."

Catherine Gretta and Philemon Solo exchanged a short, questioning look.

"So why aren't the police talking to me right now?" said Mrs. Gretta. "Instead of... a talk show host?"

"They can't prove anything yet," said Phil. "It's only a theory."

"Getting the proof is only a matter of time," said Carl. "It's a good idea to move ahead and simply raise this one question, isn't it? If dry sachets are exploding, who benefits from this?"

With a powerful gesture, Mrs. Gretta silenced him. "No one benefits from terrorism."

"Let me put it this way: who might hate you or Desi enough to start throwing bombs? Is there anyone you can think of? A competitor?"

Mrs. Gretta sighed. "This is the 21st century, Mr. Pappas. Competitors fight on the markets, not with bombs. We don't have any serious competition anyway."

"OK. Well, has anybody been bothering you recently then? You say you live like a hermit. Has anybody been trying to reach you recently in a way that looks suspicious, now that you look back at it with these explosions in mind?"

The old lady put her coffee down, got up and walked towards one of the huge windows. The glass started at floor level and went all the way up to the ceiling and was slightly tainted to keep the sunlight at bay. She stood there looking out for a while. Then she turned and looked at Phil Solo, who nodded back in a friendly way. Finally she said: "There has been someone."

Again there was silence. After a while it became sort of obvious to both the bizz jockey and the WCBN Radio manager that Mrs. Gretta was stuck in her own thoughts, they nodded to each other. Phil Solo walked towards her and put a hand on her shoulder.

"If you don't want to talk about it, we can just leave," he said.

She lifted her head to face a higher sky. The corners of her mouth, unwrinkled, almost untouched by her advancing age, pointed down for an instant — then she seemed to shake off of her whatever had been bothering her.

"That's perfectly all right, Phil. I trust you."

She turned to face him. They held hands.

The bizz jockey looked on, focusing, dedicating fifty percent of his attention to what she was saying and the other fifty percent on keeping a straight face. He had seen his boss Phil Solo seduce many women. Solo's intentions were always genuine, he felt. Yes, the man was probably a womanizer, but he was not the abusing kind. He steered away from female employees and his relationships could last for years. But he had never seen Solo so close to a woman who was many decades older, who was so powerful and so much a member of a different class. He needed to keep a straight face until he had figured out whether smiling in awe made more sense than laughing out loud.

"A long time ago, when I was very young, a teenager still, a young man fell in love with me," said Mrs. Gretta. "I was infatuated with him, and I guess for a while I was in love too. But it was never that serious for me. After a while he started to bore me and, to be honest, he started to give me the creeps. He was a fanatical boy who took himself way too serious. He used to call us Bogart-Bacall, you know, that famous movie star couple from the film noir era, that also married in real life. Then, when I terminated our relationship, he lost it."

Carl saw Mrs. Gretta look at him from the corner of her eye. "I'll wait outside," he said. Without waiting for an answer he walked out of the room.

There was no doubt in his mind that Mrs. Gretta would cry in the arms of Phil Solo as soon as he closed the door behind him. He considered that part to be Solo's problem. As long as they got the information they came for in the fist place.

As soon as the bizz jockey closed the door, Catherine started sobbing quietly and she allowed Philemon to put his arms around her for comfort.

"This man... I have been able to keep him at a great distance," she said, when she had regained control. "But only now that I talk about him to you, do realize that I have been keeping that distance for almost half a century."

Phil was so shocked that he almost let her go. "This man... has been bothering you for fifty years?"

"No. Not while my husband was still alive. But for the past couple of years, he has become a problem."

She moved out of his embrace, away from him. She needed to reinforce herself altogether. "It doesn't matter. You have to forget this happened, Philemon. I am not afraid of this man. I also find it hard to believe what Pappas is saying: that he is putting explosives into our dry sachets. Why on earth?"

"Revenge, maybe," said Solo.

She straightened her back and her looks hardened again, to their previous settings of coldness. "If you believe there is a possibility that any of this is true, you can tell your bizz jockey he can exert pressure to whatever extent he feels necessary. He has my blessing. But if one word about me and this... former lover of mine comes out, I will sue you until I go bankrupt."

To that, Phil Solo smiled broadly. "It will never come to that, Catherine. Trust me."

He walked towards the door. "In that case I will sue Pappas myself."

===

While Pappas was being briefed by Solo on their way to the car, a subway train rushed through one of the tunnels deep below the city. A woman sat on one of the seats. There weren't many people in the wagon with her, since the morning was already well on the way and most people were already in their downtown offices. She could smell the fresh odor of her new laptop bag she had purchased the previous weekend.

Annoying, she thought, the smell of new stuff. Now I'll have to answer stupid questions in the office about why I've bought a new bag and why I've chosen this stupid model and why I didn't follow their advice and buy a cheap one online in some faraway low wages country, manufactured, no doubt, by underpaid adolescents.

This was exactly the bag she needed and she didn't want to talk about it.

And she wasn't going to either, because the whole thing exploded before the train reached the next subway station. The blast ripped through the wagon and its occupants, its force blew out the windows and its heat melted the paint of the interior and turned the chairs into dripping works of surreal art. It didn't derail the train, but it caused a fire in the tunnel nonetheless and people died, and it was going to be all over the news.

Seventeen

Hitomi Sakamoto stood beyond the studio window. She looked straight at Carl and, with her right hand, made the "zipper" movement across her lips. It was a brisk movement and couldn't be misunderstood.

Carl Pappas sighed.

The Boardroom, the world's number one business talk radio show, was broadcast across the globe in various timeslots, depending on the local time zone. But it could always be listened to through the internet while it was broadcasted live from the WCBN Radio building. Many business people among its audience were up at night anyway. The lights never go down on Dubai, or Moscow, or Shanghai, and megacities alike.

That evening the show opened with a slightly somber mood, right after a news bulletin that announced three explosions in the city and the surrounding area.

And right after a couple of commercials, of course, for clothing, men's fragrances and a new deodorant that strongly suggested immense success for anyone who decided to buy and use it. Carl Pappas, the bizz jockey, could easily have joked about that particular commercial, but not that night. His mood was way too serious and so the show took off the way it always did, but this time without an opening joke.

"It's eleven o'clock," the radio station voice barked. "The city is dark, but the fire burns. It burns in the offices. It burns on Wall Street. It burns in the City. It burns on the Bund. It burns in Dubai. It burns in the factories and power plants. And it burns within us. Because we are the business and we all need redemption. This is the hour of delusion and today's truth. This is The Boardroom. Here is your prophet, the buddy and the bodyguard of every CEO, the Don Juan of every business babe. Here is the world's one and only buzz jockey. Here is your BJ: Carl Pappas!"

There was never any mention of his other, unofficial profession, that of a radio detective. He sure felt like one tonight, but both Phil Solo and Hitomi Sakamoto had insisted on him keeping his mouth shut about the alleged connection between the explosions and the Desi factory. He would have to wait for Lieutenant Carlsberg to come up with results.

"Catherine Gretta will sue our station as soon as we say anything about this," Phil had warned him. "You will be the one who breaks the news, but not now, Carl."

So that was that. Pappas looked at Hitomi again, who raised her head and zipped up her lips once again. Then he smiled. *Crazy woman.*

"I don't know about you folks," he began, "but I'm a bit down tonight. There's a lunatic throwing explosives around our city. I sympathize with you if you are at the other end of the world where all is quiet, but here it's pretty depressing. Are we facing another terrorist threat or a renegade psycho killer from the 1970s? Because that's when we had those. *Are you listening, fool? Blowing up subway trains is sooo last century!*"

Phil Solo shook his head from behind another window and Hitomi could be seen making a remark to the sound engineer sitting beside her, Don Wozniak.

But the radio detective was feeling a good rant emerge, like a rogue wave, and he was going to ride this one out.

===

Lieutenant Carlsberg was not amused. "That" woman had turned up unexpected and he didn't like that one bit. He could appreciate a woman who made a stand, but Hitomi Sakamoto was too much for him right now. There were all these factory workers on strike, there was the angry Desi management, the police chief was pissed off and the mayor was passing on pressure from higher places, and all that was dripping downwards towards Carlsberg.

Dripping? It was pouring!

On top of all that the sound of jazz was echoing across the premises. Some idiot had turned on the speaker system to make the whole damn thing sound like some fun picnic.

But it wasn't. It was a dangerous affair. If there were explosive sachets shipped from this place, things might turn ugly.

"If all these people walk in and out all the time," he said to a worker who seemed to be in charge of a whole group, "then how can you be certain there's no trespassing going on?"

"Trespassing?" the man shouted.

There was a lot of noise, so the shouting wasn't unfriendly or anything.

"Are all these people," — Carlsberg jerked his head in a circular motion — "allowed to be here?"

"How the hell should I know?" the man barked back.

But he couldn't escape Carlsberg's intense and irritated stare.

"OK, I see your point. I don't think anyone can vouch for all of these people all at once. But there's nothing to steal here, you know. It's just industrial machines too heavy to move and tons of desiccant."

"Des... what?"

"Desiccant. The stuff that goes into the dry sachets."

This is pointless, Carlsberg thought.

Fortunately, Hitomi Sakamoto turned up and grabbed his arm. "Come," she yelled.

They walked away from the crowd and turned a corner, where the sound of the speaker system was reduced to a comfortable level.

"The foreman, John Bremen, is gone," Hitomi said.

"How do you know?" Carlsberg growled. "There's hundreds of people here."

"Trust me, he's gone. I asked a couple of people and they all say the same thing, they haven't seen him since last night. So, I called his wife and..."

Carlsberg hissed. "You did wh... You called his wife? Who asked you? Listen, you have to talk to me if you hear anything, got that? This is an official investigation. Did Pappas send you?"

"Don't you want to know what his wife said?" whispered

Hitomi.

"For crying out loud, woman, talk to me before I hear it on the radio!"

She smiled — Carlsberg had rarely seen that on her face before: a smile. "She said she called the police station this morning to report her husband missing."

Carlsberg didn't blush. He was the kind of man who thought that blushing and smoking look good on young people and at least he'd got ridden of the blushing part.

"Didn't they tell you at the station, Lieutenant?"

Before the Lieutenant could grab his cell phone to call the police station downtown, Hitomi grabbed his elbow and pulled him along. "I need you to see something, Lieutenant." He found himself intrigued by Hitomi's enthusiasm and energy; even though following her would obviously prove to be a total waste of his precious time.

"You must have this train inspected, Lieutenant."

He looked at the bulk. It stood there as it had been standing there before and there was absolutely nothing going on and no one around. Carlsberg decided to go along with the idea of having Hitomi Sakamoto as an assistant inspector and just to ask the right questions. "Give me one good reason to put a team on it, Mrs. Sakamoto."

"Uh, that'll be Miss Sakamoto. I think it's odd that a train this large stands here idly."

"On the contrary. It's a factory loading zone. It makes perfect sense."

"Freight trains are needed. And if they're not, they are parked in zones where they can be put to active duty at a moment's notice. This one has been overlooked, no doubt.

And there's another thing."

Carlsberg decided not to sigh.

"It has been standing here since the day the strike began."

"The railway company probably thought it best not to interfere. Besides, the Desi people are paying for that train anyway, so who cares?"

"You do," said Hitomi. She would have loved to sound extra-serious, but that was simply out of the question for someone who sounded serious all the time anyway.

"Come on, Miss Saigon... excuse me, Miss Sakamoto," Carlsberg said as he pushed her forward, away from the train platform. "You've given me a more important lead on Mr. John Bremen. I need you to tell me exactly what his wife said to you. Can you tell me again?"

===

"I won't certainly not tell you again," said Catherine Gretta. "Haven't you heard quite enough of this awful affair?"

"There's stuff you haven't told me," Phil Solo said softly, "and you don't need to. I'm just... worried. People are dying and I don't see why you refuse to open up about this suspect."

"He's not officially a suspect, is he?"

"Not yet, but he will be real soon."

"He leaves me stone cold," Catharine said, aggressively.

"What did he do?"

"He deliberately caused a plane to crash. Three people died. He and I survived — by some ridiculous sleight of hand. He was deformed, but he survived nevertheless. I was rescued by angels, no doubt. Without any injuries."

"Other than psychic."

"You think I'm traumatized, is that it?"

"I don't know. You're... evasive."

"Wouldn't you be if you broke up with a boyfriend forty years ago and he got so angry he crashed a plane to get his revenge?

"Was he sent to prison?"

"No. There was no proof. Also... it was too outrageous for the authorities to believe to be true. But that's all in the past. Here, you read this."

She took an envelope from her desk.

"You keep his letters, then?"

"No, they just keep coming, that's all," said Catherine. "I throw them away without opening them, but this one arrived this morning and I thought it would be a good idea if you read it. You're obnoxious; a know-it-all. What do you know about these things, Philémon? What do you know about a crazy, insane love?"

He didn't answer. Instead he looked at the letter. The first lines were a poem.

Broke the glass in the dishwater
Your lips blood red on a shard
Threw the whole shaboodle into the dustbin
Early next morning I took the bin to the street, wounded my hand bloody by your lips
Even in silence, your kiss is still dangerous

"Oh Catherine," said Phil Solo, "haven't you tried to get this man locked up in an institution? For stalking?"

"He didn't bother me for most of my married years," said Catherine. "It wasn't until after my husband died that he really got loose. Then he started to write this awful stuff. And this is... mild."

She poured herself a glass of Scotch. "Anyway, I won't bow for a stalker. Not for strikers, not for stalkers. Not this lady."

Eighteen

Mach One sat close to the windows of the bar on the eightieth floor. Behind him the city lay in the afternoon sun, soundless beyond the thick windows, and motionless but for the silhouette of an aircraft descending. He had turned his back to it all, because he didn't care about the view right now. He was taking another assignment from his favorite client, the bizz jockey of WCBN Radio, and he was all ears.

Those ears were covered partly by his hair, flattened from wearing his old hat, the one he desperately wanted to replace but could not find the time for. His hat and his long coat, just as old, were thrown over one of the chairs casually so that he could keep an eye on them. He liked to keep an eye on basically everything; that's what made him so good at what he did.

He stroked his mustache while he listened to Carl Pappas. He repositioned the hairs a bit, so that they wouldn't cover the vertical scar on his lip. He also squeezed his battered nose as if he was trying to avoid sneezing. All in all, he was a man who was always doing something.

"Now, Mrs. Gretta remembers him only by his first name,"

said Pappas.

"Are you saying you actually met Catherine Gretta?" said Mach One, sounding genuinely in awe.

"Uh, yes? Is that... special?"

"She's notoriously unavailable. She's been living behind a curtain for decades now. You may not remember this, but in her younger days, Catherine Gretta was a starlet, child of famous and wealthy parents, born into the stratosphere of power and fame. She was well on her way becoming a Broadway star when she suddenly withdrew at a very young age. She's been avoiding the limelight ever since. Even while being married, she stayed in the background while her husband acquired many businesses. She is extremely wealthy but she still actively guards her late husbands estate. True love, if you ask me."

Carl was silent for a moment. Then he said: "Really, Mach, I'd rather not ask. This is an urgent matter, if you don't mind."

"All your matter is urgent, Carl," said Mach One. "It goes without saying. It's just... unusual."

"When she was very young, she was in love with a dude called Fernando. You must find him and check out his current state of affairs. Can you do that for me?"

"Sure. She doesn't... remember his last name?"

"Either she doesn't or she won't. He... caused a plane to crash."

Mach One's mouth fell open. His hand lowered to his lap so his full two-part mustache was revealed. "He did what?"

"She was on it."

Suddenly Mach One was all movement, hovering over the

table, wringing his hands. "I love crazy cases, man. You can count on me."

"Good," said Pappas. "Do you want me to wait here till you report back?"

"Funny man," said Mach One, shoving his chair backwards and getting up, grabbing his hat and coat. "But I can take a good joke. You stay here and get lunch, while I dive into it. Keep your cell phone close at hand."

Carl Pappas turned and looked after Mach One, who rushed towards the elevator. He smiled. It was a crazy case and a crazy man was on it.

===

"You are all choir boys," said Catherine Gretta with a snarling voice not uncommon to her outside her private life.

At least her audience was used to it. They were the Board of Directors of the Desi Corporation and they were sitting on the top floor of the company's office building in the city. Outside the sun had provided a happy sky, but even if the windows hadn't been tainted, they would have been oblivious to the view because of current events. Their suits were sharp, their ties were straightened, the women had perfect hairdos — but none of that made any difference now that they were facing the wall. It was a dead end for them.

"You think you are safe from angry workers who are too far away to strangle you all," Mrs. Gretta continued, "and you are probably right. They are not going to march over here and come to you. And if they did, they'd find this room empty anyway because you would all make a run for it. Go to the roof and board your corporate helicopter." She looked them all in the eye, one by one, all sixteen of them. "Shame on you."

"We have negotiated for months and there is simply no solution that will satisfy both parties," said Jonathan Grosmont. "John Bremen has us by the balls."

"He has *you* by the balls," a woman said. She looked like a younger version of Gretta, slim and tall and with long black hair in a ponytail. Her suit shone in the vague sunlight when she got up. "I'm sorry Jonathan, but I can see it no other way."

"Oh. So now you're turning on me?"

"None of us were present at the negotiations, Jonathan," a man said. His hairs stood straight up as if static electricity was pulling at him. Through his thick glasses his large eyes gazed innocently into the world. "We're all too busy bringing Desi forward, coming up with cost-efficient new ways to produce and package and transport, while you..."

"Enough with the chitchat," said Catherine Gretta. "You people have had all the time in the world. I'm going there myself and fix this once and for all."

A whining, high-pitched voice came from the far end of the table. A man with large glasses and a pale complexion, balding, sat there with his hand spread out on the table. He looked at his hands. "That is a very bad idea, Mrs. Gretta."

A few of the members inhaled a large amount of air, as if they were preparing for a shortage. They watched silently as Mrs. Gretta walked across the room towards the man who had just spoken.

When she had reached him, she said: "And why is that, Rocco?"

The man got up.

Not that it mattered, because Mrs. Gretta was so much taller that he still had to look up. But he stood his ground nonetheless. "Because of all these rumors that someone is putting explosives in our sachets to hurt you. Not the company, but you."

Some face muscles in Catherine's face betrayed the fact that she was grinding her teeth. "Well, that's an honest opinion, Rocco. I can't argue with rumors. Go on."

"I think you should sell your shares, Mrs. Gretta."

The other fifteen members started to talk simultaneously. The whole room was filled with noise all of a sudden.

But Catherine Gretta didn't pay attention to that. She moved closer to the little man. "It's a good thing I know you, Rocco. Other people might think you have lost your mind."

"Think about it, Mrs. Gretta. Desi can't handle a strike of this magnitude and deal with a terrorist at the same time."

"There is no proof that these bombings are connected to Desi. Nor to me."

"That's just an argument, Mrs. Gretta. If this is not dealt with very quickly, it will be the undoing of the Desi Corporation. You have other business interests, but for the people who work here, it is the brink of disaster."

Catherine raised her head. "You've made your point. I am personally taking charge of the situation and will end this. If I fail, I suppose your advice is worth some consideration. Good day."

By the time she reached the door of the boardroom, the silence had ended again.

===

Later that day, the sun took off to see another part of the world, leaving behind a pink light. Catherine Gretta looked at it from the roof of the Desi headquarters, while Philemon Solo looked at her.

"I like that color," said Catherine. "It suggests that all is well with the world. Of course you could also say it will turn blood red in a few moments — but if you forget about that it looks innocent. Doesn't it?"

She looked at Solo, who said nothing.

"Oh you're young, you're probably more interested in the dark that follows, the wild night, when there are women to be chased, or the full daylight when there's business to be done. You don't care about pink."

"Not really, no," he said. "Besides, if you want to give it a meaning, I'd go for the blood red. It all looks ominous for you, Catherine. There's no way you can deny that."

"I'm tired of it all, Philemon," said Catherine. "I only inherited the Desi Corporation from my late husband. It's only one of many companies I own and I merely visit the board meetings once a year. I can't even sell Desi off now — its shares are making a nosedive. These two problems need to be fixed first. Then I'll get rid of it, if ever."

"If there's someone trying to destroy Desi, things can become dangerous. You can't just walk to the factory like that, Cath."

"I won't, Phil. I won't. Just you wait and see. Now... be a nice young executive and pour me a drink."

The pink light was quickly turning dark red.

===

The security people of the Desi factory were extremely unhappy with the way things were going. It all started with the rising noise level; the workers on strike had started talking in more aggressive and louder tones, and were having more and more heated arguments amongst themselves. Apparently they were growing restless, unhappy with the results of the negotiations. They were also angry about the rumor that the foreman and strike leader John Bremen had gotten cold feet and ran away.

But most likely they were primarily growing tired of the waiting, the seemingly endless hours of hanging around and the growing uncertainty of their incomes. The prospect of having to go home and explain the downfall of the factory and the loss of their jobs was unacceptable.

For the first time, a small riot had broken out in the restaurant when that evening's dinner — a regular pasta with a tomato sauce — was being served from the counter. A huge worker had asked for more "Berlusconi sauce" instead of Bolognese, and then some other tall, thin guy had hollered "You making fun of my country?", to which the first man had answered "I couldn't if I tried". Then they were at each other's throats and at least one table, two chairs and a whole casserole full of spaghetti had been compromised in the fight.

The security people had been able to prevent the fight from spreading, but afterwards they had decided to call for backup before things got any worse.

Nineteen

The men and women hanging around the Desi factory gate were taking turns. There were a couple of thousand workers employed here and they obviously couldn't all be there at the same time. So only a few hundred were present and they did their own cooking in the factory restaurant, they barbecued out in the open, chairs had been brought out, and there were makeshift beds inside the factory — but in general the mood was gloomy. They had been on strike for days now and nothing had been achieved. They were getting restless. They were working class heroes, people who wanted to get back to work.

By now they not only blamed Jonathan Grosmont for failing to meet their demands, but also John Bremen, who had mysteriously disappeared. None of them bought the police statement about the man being declared missing.

"He ran off," someone said and after a while they all said it. "He shit his pants."

It wasn't just the worth of the Desi Corporation that was taking a nosedive as a result of the explosions — which had by now become an issue in the media and the public opinion —

and the strike. The mood among the workers was rapidly deteriorating. Some spoke of a march towards the city, where the company's headquarters stood.

Then, out of the blue, dark limousines turned up at the gate and the security people announced the arrival of the factory's owner, Mrs. Catherine Gretta. Out of nowhere, TV cameras showed up and the circus was complete. There was shouting and hollering, and for a moment the security people — who had so far maintained friendly relations with the striking workers — feared violence, but then a small miracle occurred.

Out of the first car, Mrs. Catherine Gretta emerged.

The crowd fell silent.

There wasn't a single person present who knew this woman. She came from a no man's land, but it was immediately clear to all that she was important and that she came with a purpose.

Without any hesitation she walked through the gate, right into the mass of workers. From the other car, men in black suits ran after her, confused by her sudden and unannounced movements.

Everybody looked on completely surprised. They all waited for something to happen.

When she reached the center of the crowd, she stopped.

"Good people of Desi," she said, loud and clear, "can you all hear me?"

A massive murmur moved around her like a wave.

"You are all in danger," she said.

Around her, the men in black suits had posted, some with a finger at the hearing device in their ears, but they looked silly and redundant nevertheless. They raised their eyebrows when she said the people were in danger. More unexpected stuff, which they didn't like. Security is all about tightening your grip on the status quo, and then sort of keeping it in limbo.

"There are rumors of explosive devices in the dry sachets you make," she spoke with all her force. "There are threats from other countries who want to jerk away your jobs across the border and leave you unemployed. There are competitors who threaten to produce the same stuff you are manufacturing, and sell it for less money. There is the threat from the Desi Corporation to whip more labor out of you."

The crowd burst into a roaring cheer.

Catherine Gretta waved and it was quiet again.

"And last but not least, you are threatened by yourself, for stalling all negotiations as if it were still 1974 and you could do whatever you please and have the union behind you forever. The people who are representing you are not doing their job right. And I heard your main man, Mr. John Bremen, has left the building."

A low humming returned.

"Therefore I have come here myself to take charge of this ridiculous situation. My late husband founded the company you work for and I am not going to stand by and see it ripped to shreds. Not by you, not by the Desi management and not by a terrorist. Please stand by me. Let's end this charade."

In the background, Hitomi Sakamoto and Phil Solo smiled in the afternoon sun, as the crowd burst into cheering. People came forward to pat Catherine on the back, and she disappeared out of view.

"She sounds like a union leader," said Hitomi. "Not like a

former starlet who has been hiding from the media for decades."

"You don't know the half of it," grumbled Phil. "Ah, there's Lieutenant Carlsberg."

They waited for the policeman.

"There's a large police force present now," the Lieutenant said. "We're actually thinking about sending everybody home, just to be on the safe side. But there's still not enough to go on and, to be honest, we don't want to be responsible for breaking a strike."

"John Bremen still hasn't been found?" asked Hitomi.

"No."

"They still think he just ran off?"

"Yes," said Carlsberg. "And the mood is getting grimmer all the time. It could turn sour any moment, one little flame and the whole situation will explode."

"The owner's arrival seems to be having a calming effect," said Solo. "Well, I'm going inside, there's stuff I need to do."

"Are you here as a reporter?" asked Carlsberg. "I mean, what exactly are you doing here?"

"I'm a personal friend of Mrs. Gretta," said Phil. "I'm going to stick around a bit and make sure she's all right."

"There are dozens of policemen, the entire security force from the factory plus she brought her own security people," said Hitomi. "Which part of her security will you be handling?"

Phil Solo smiled at Lieutenant Carlsberg. "Charming, don't you think?"

The man didn't answer.

That earned him a point on Hitomi's scale, no doubt,

because as they watched Solo walk away, she said: "I like a man who can keep his mouth shut at the right time."

Carlsberg felt it would be better to say nothing in response.

Twenty

"I don't have time to go inside the restaurant now," said Carl Pappas.

They were standing on the parking lot of the *Gulag* in the early morning. Carl had waited outside for Mach One to arrive — much to the annoyance of Kate Yekaterina, the restaurant's owner and primary servant. She had come out to inquire if anything was the matter, but he had sent her back in without any explanation.

"You are a funny man," was Mach's response. "They call me Mach One because I'm fast, but do you actually know why I am so fast? Why do I go through all the trouble to come up with information faster than everybody else, including all official secret services?"

"I haven't the foggiest," the bizz jockey replied.

"If I get the job done faster than average," said Mach, "I save me and my client time, which we can then spend sitting down and drink some coffee and talk like normal human beings."

"You are not a normal human being, Mach. I don't know your name, I don't know how you operate, I know nothing about you. Can we please get to the point? Just this time, OK? I promise you a bit of chitchat next time."

The ruffled private eye rubbed his chin and looked across the river. The *Gulag* was built on the river bank, rising high above the water that flowed through the heart of the city, as it had been doing since before the city was even there.

"That's OK, bizz jockey," said Mach. "I've found this for you. This Fernando character, he lives a very withdrawn life, has been doing that for decades. The story about the air disaster confirms; he has been injured to the extent that his face is deformed and he rarely shows himself in public. He is very wealthy nonetheless. Lives outside the city in a large mansion."

"Anything else? I mean, is that it?"

"No, the best is yet to come, Mr. Bizz Jockey."

===

Lieutenant Carlsberg thought the scene was unique.

He was looking at the large crowd standing outside the factory. Hundreds of men and women in the morning sun, their feet wet from the morning dew in the grass they had crossed, smoke rising from either cigarettes or their breaths evaporating in the cold air. They had all assembled by the train platform. Behind them, the abandoned freight train stood motionless.

Under their feet were more rails.

In front of them stood Catherine Gretta on a concrete platform a meter high, connected to the far end of the factory building.

In the distance, stood the security people and the police. Also on the platform, their backs against the factory wall, the security people had lined up. The crowd was noisy and unhappy.

"Don't you think the police force is way too small to intervene when this gets out of hand?" whispered Hitomi in Carlsberg's ear.

She stood extremely close to him — although everybody on the platform stood extremely close to each other, she couldn't help it — and he smiled.

"It's all been taken care of," he whispered, yes, he jumped at the opportunity to whisper in the Japanese woman's ear, hidden somewhere in that lush fountain of black hair. "There's a unit standing by."

"I hope they're not too far away," said Hitomi. "It doesn't feel good. It doesn't feel good at all."

===

"Mrs. Gretta's old lover Fernando's full name is Fernando Monterrey," said Mach One, "and he is the owner of a string of businesses. One of these businesses is actually the largest international competitor of the Desi Corporation. They also manufacture dry sachets for use in bags and stuff."

Carl pushed out a sigh that became a scream. "And you are saying Catherine Gretta doesn't know this? I can't believe it. She's a liar!"

"Oh, but she may be unaware of it. This competing company, well, it is located in India. This Fernando Monterrey is not a very visible man. He is also not the CEO or the

Chairman or anything. He only purchased it a few years ago so it is on his portfolio. I did find out that his company has been relentlessly competing with Desi in the past two years. It has the appearance of an attempt to run Desi into the ground."

"Another nosedive then," said Carl, more to himself than to Mach One.

"None of this sheds any light on the exploding sachets though," said Mach. "So I have made a theory for you. The strike began a several hours before the first explosion. That could mean that whoever planted these explosives inside the factory, is still on the premises."

"I don't see how that's logical, Mach."

"It's a theory," said Mach. "If you're in a hurry, let's not get into it any further. I have not been able to link Fernando Monterrey to these explosions. There isn't much to go on anyway. But it is possible that the terrorist was expecting to get out easily and then suddenly found himself in the middle of a strike. That shakes up the safety routines at that factory and he may have been unable to leave He cannot get out without being seen. There are hundreds of people all over the place."

"A crowd gives him a nice cover, I'd say. Nobody will ask him who he is."

"Could be. But if you're a terrorist you don't want to be discovered in a crowd that could potentially lynch you for it."

"Point taken. Listen, thanks Mach, I'm off. We'll call later."

Carl walked off towards his car.

"You be careful now, bizz jockey. This is not a radio show where you get to kick ass from behind a microphone. There's a real lunatic on the loose and crowds on strike tend to be angry with the media."

The bizz jockey saluted Mach One with a smile, touching his imaginary cowboy hat with two fingers as he got into his car.

Twenty-one

"You'd look good in a mansion," Carl Pappas said to Phil Solo as they waited in the living room of Fernando Monterrey's house.

The room was immense, they couldn't even see if there was a door on the other end or if it was just a painting. Beyond the windows a lawn stretched towards a wall of rhododendrons, the only thing they could see of Monterrey's vast estate.

"Ordering pretty maids around, confusing the hell out of them, making dubious remarks like 'Oh, I'd looove to taste your fruit'."

"Surely you don't hold me for a man who misbehaves," said Solo. "Anyway, these mansions are not for me. They're all too far from the comforts of the city. No bars. No restaurants. No corporate headquarters and no airport nearby. Just people, bored to death, behind their bushes and walls."

"Is Catherine Gretta bored?"

"I don't know. She's not boring, that's for sure. But she wants to live private, and that's easier out here. She doesn't want to be locked up in some penthouse."

And then, indeed, the painting at the far end of the room turned out to be a door. It was opened and closed very quickly and a tall man walked towards them with a speed that grabbed their attention; was this man in a hurry or did he always walk like that?

As soon as they all shook hands and the man introduced himself, they knew: here was a man who lived in another world, where time moved faster.

"Mr. Carl Pappas, the bizz jockey, and his boss. The honor, gentleman, is entirely mine. I am Fernando Monterrey, at your service."

His handshake was powerful, a cool hand and a fast pumping grip.

They gazed at him unabashedly.

Fernando Monterrey was a tall man with a South American look. He was handsome the way a southern Casanova can be handsome: a face with dark eyes and even darker eyebrows, white teeth, a strong chin, a nice tan and shining black hair combed back in a way that would cost Richard Gere two hours with makeup on a movie set. He was also thin and athletic. The only thing that marked him out was the speed at which he moved and spoke. It was eerie.

Fernando Monterrey spread his arms elegantly. "Gentlemen, be seated. Coffee is coming. And feel free to examine my face up close." He smiled when he said that last line.

Pappas and Solo sat down.

"I do apologize," said Carl. "I was indeed expecting to see a man damaged by a severe air disaster. I'm sorry, that was rude."

"You are two well-informed gentlemen," said Monterrey, still smiling a smile that looked like it was there to stay. "One doesn't come across your species very often. These days there's hardly anyone around who knows about this."

There was a short silence. They were expecting the man to ask how they had found out — but he didn't.

"It is many decades ago. Surgery has advanced to such an extent that they can repair almost anything these days. But I can assure you my wounds are still there and they hurt twenty-four hours a day."

"Is that why you stay out of the public eye?" asked Carl.

"Yes. I am never comfortable, you see," said Monterrey as he got up from his chair, waved the woman who came in with coffee to carry on, and started to walk through the room. "For me, there is always pain. You don't want to be in a plane on your way to Sydney or Mumbai in my condition. It is best to stay at home, where there's always medical care, you see?"

By the time the woman had gone again, he came back from his walk towards the other end of the room and smiled again. "So I am of no use to your radio show, Mr. Pappas. I stay in the background and I will not appear on your show. But that is not what you came for, is it?"

"No, it is not," said Pappas, raising his voice to his recognizable holler. "Mr. Monterrey, I have a question to ask you."

The man sat down again. He didn't sit quietly, but he sat. "Go ahead."

"One of the world's greatest coincidences must be the fact that you own a large corporation that is the biggest and only significant competitor of the Desi Corporation, owned by your former fiancé, Mrs. Catherine Gretta. Wouldn't you say?"

Monterrey's face showed nothing. He leaned forward a bit. "Wouldn't I say what, Mr. Pappas?"

"Wouldn't you say that is one of the world's greatest coincidences? Come on, Mr. Monterrey. You crashed a plane because you couldn't take it that she ended your relationship. Now, forty years later, you own a company in the same line of business. You have also been sending her letters recently."

Fernando Monterrey sighed and got up again. "You are gravely mistaken," he said, as he started his nervous pacing again. "Perhaps Mrs. Gretta has told you this nonsense. Why would I crash a plane when I'm in it myself?"

"Everybody else is dead, so it's her word against yours, isn't it?" said Solo.

"Yes it is," shouted Monterrey. "Like it has been for all these years, after I was acquitted by the authorities. I live with the scars, she doesn't. What are you really saying? That I am trying to destroy her by competing with her? That I am stalking her through the mail? Please tell me, Carl, Phil, if you allow me to call you that, please tell me why I have waited forty years for my revenge. Huh? Can you tell me that?"

He stopped right in front of them and looked Carl in the eye. "Answer me!" Then he stepped to Phil, and repeated his shouted order. "Answer me!"

"Relax, Mr. Monterrey," said Phil. "Never mind that you're in a police file. Never mind that you've been on trial. But it is obvious that Catherine Gretta is in grave danger. If you once loved her, please tell us what you know."

There was no doubt about it: Fernando Monterrey's laugh was entirely hysterical. It reminded Phil Solo of the comic books he read in his childhood years, about lunatics with painted faces who tried to kill the hero forevermore. It reminded Carl Pappas of his radio show, because he got crazy phone calls on so many occasions.

When he stopped laughing, he even seemed exhausted. "I did love Catherine Gretta once, but the whole idea seems preposterous to me now. That woman... she deserves no love. She is not worthy of it. So if that is all you came for, to accuse me of all this — I bid you farewell."

He turned around and walked off.

"The same to you," yelled Carl Pappas, just before the man left the room.

===

On the platform, Catherine Gretta made an historic speech. What started out as a potentially violent situation, suddenly took a turn for the better.

"When I came here, I was probably as angry as all of you. I don't know, angry at you, angry at the management, angry because all of this couldn't be negotiated properly. Then I walked in the midst of you people and it dawned on me: you aren't standing here for fun!"

The hundreds of strikers started to cheer. When the noise faded, Gretta resumed her speech.

"So, I decided here and now that as long as we're not going to have any fun anyway, we might as well get it over with!"

She talked in a loud, powerful voice and the crowd burst into another short bout of cheers. Next to her stood a man with a megaphone, but she had refused to use it.

"I'm used to working with what we've got. What we got here is a trainload full of dry sachets. That's worth quite a bit of money. We are going to use the profits from the contents of this train to improve the working conditions and the working hours."

Dumbfounded, the crowd turned heads and looked at the freight train. It was a very long train. There were at least fifty wagons full of merchandise.

So another round of cheering rolled across the platform.

"In addition to that, I am going to personally meet your demands and add ten percent of the profits to boost your pension fund."

This time they were too surprised to react. But that didn't bother Mrs. Gretta.

"At this particular junction, that will not improve the position of Desi from a competitive point of view, but what the hell. It is important that you feel wanted and needed. When you trust Desi again, I trust you people to help fight the international competition. Which is fierce, but I am confident you can manage." She pointed at the crowd. "And there you are," she finally said, as a sort of closure, because talking to angry crowds was not what she was trained to do.

As the cheering started once again, Catherine Gretta grabbed the megaphone to get the attention back and start answering questions from the crowd, Lieutenant Carlsberg looked at Hitomi beside him and caught her staring across the workers' heads towards the train.

"What's the matter?" he said to her. There was no need to whisper; there was too much noise anyhow.

"He's in the train," said Hitomi, almost breathless. She bent over so close to Carlsberg that for a second he was confused about her motives. Then he heard her say: "Look at the eleventh wagon."

===

The door of the wagon was opened slightly, perhaps no more than five centimeters. But it was enough for the man with the scar to look through it and watch Catherine Gretta on the platform being cheered at by the crowd. He scanned the scene carefully and after a while realized that the police force present was huge. When at some point he saw a man and a woman on the platform, standing behind Gretta, look straight at him, and talk conspicuously to each other, he started to panic. When one of them waved to a uniformed policeman and talked to him, he decided he had no time to lose.

For days he had been hiding out. First in the train. Then when he found out it wouldn't be leaving for a while, he retreated to the factory. After a while he decided that the freight train was still the safest place to hide, so he moved to one of the wagons. By now he was exhausted — he had found some food in the factory and in the locomotive, but he was running out of supplies. He dared not walk the terrain for fear of being discovered, so he was in many ways a trapped animal. His connection with the outside world was gone.

But he had the stuff that victories are made of. And he had plenty of it.

Twenty-two

Carl Pappas reached the scene just as it was getting out of hand. When he walked onto the platform, the crowd was leaving towards the area around the main entrance. There were police and security people, a few workers, Mrs. Gretta with her security guys and Carlsberg and Sakamoto.

Then the door from one of the freight train wagons opened and a man appeared.

"Listen up!" he shouted. "Check this out."

He threw something out of the train, to a place where nobody stood. It hit the ground, right in front of the platform, and exploded with a mighty bang. The area shuddered; the train hollered with a metal echo and a cloud of gray smoke rose up.

Everyone automatically covered their ears because the explosion was painful.

While they stood there, bent over, confused, the man jumped from the train and ran towards the platform where he reached Mrs. Gretta. "I got more!" he yelled.

Then he grabbed the stunned lady by an arm and jerked her off the platform, towards the train. As they moved, he threw something again, and everybody ducked to avoid another bang.

By the time they reasserted themselves, the unknown man and Mrs. Gretta had already disappeared into the train.

Complete chaos reigned. Because the three security forces — the police, the Desi security and the private team of Mrs. Gretta — had made no arrangements for dealing with such an emergency, there was confusion about who was in charge. Shouting and arguing ensued, with some people approaching the train only to be called back again.

Next a roaring noise erupted.

"He's starting the train," yelled Hitomi Sakamoto.

"You can't be serious!" said Carlsberg, and he started running towards the locomotive at the end.

But they couldn't get to it. The unknown man threw explosives one by one, and the message was clear.

Meanwhile the train indeed started moving.

"We have one advantage!" shouted Carl Pappas in Carlsberg's ears.

"I can't think of anything!" answered Carlsberg.

"The locomotive is behind the train, so he can't disconnect it and take off quickly. He'll have to push the entire train in front of him. That gives us time."

Carlsberg didn't like that last line. "Time to do what, bizz jockey?"

But the bizz jockey was already running.

All security forces stood back as ordered. Obviously the hostage situation would hardly improve if dozens of security and police officers were to jump on the freight train.

The terrorist threw one exploding sachet after another from the locomotive cockpit. Thick clouds from these explosions drifted alongside the train, giving it a sinister look, as if the whole thing was burning. It also created the right amount of chaos, as the train started to gain speed and crashed through the fence leaving the factory premises behind.

By that time, Carl Pappas and Lieutenant Carlsberg had jumped on the train, somewhere in that fog, outside of the terrorist's view.

They stood on a ladder between two carriages, coughing from the toxic smoke they had inhaled.

"That was a stupid thing to do, bizz jockey," grumbled Carlsberg. "To jump in the middle of a hostage situation."

"I'm not going to stand there and see a train take off with Catherine Gretta in the hands of that idiot," Carl Pappas said, panting. "At least now we know whoever that guy is, he's not Fernando Monterrey. In a way, that's a relief."

"I hope I'm not going to find out that you guys have been obstructing justice," said Carlsberg.

"Not that I'm aware of," said Carl. "We did some investigating ourselves and were about to share that with you."

"And when exactly was that going to be?"

Carl started to climb up the ladder.

"Bizz jockey!"

"I don't think the man even has a gun! What do you think?" he said, pausing and bending downwards towards Carlsberg.

"He has a shitload of explosives. I'd say that's worth more

than a gun," snapped the Lieutenant. He leaned over towards the edge of the wagon and looked back at the factory, that was now quickly disappearing in the distance. "What I don't understand is why nobody else took any action." He reached inside his coat, took out his cell phone and started making calls.

In the locomotive cockpit, Catherine Gretta sat on a chair looking at the man driving the train. She didn't know him but she had decided to attack him from the very start.

"Are you finally through throwing those terrible explosives out the window, young man?" she snapped. "By now they must have understood the point you're so bluntly trying to make."

"Shut up," said the man, for the umpteenth time. "I am not sure how much more of your talking I can stand." He looked at the five monitors at the freight train exterior and the route ahead. There was nothing to be seen but wagons speeding through the forest.

He sat back to relax for a moment. "I swear you are driving me insane. If you keep this up, I am going to shut you up, old lady."

Twenty-three

Right at the back of Fernando Monterrey's mansion was a large terrace and an enormous lawn. From the afternoon sky a helicopter was descending on the grass. The rhododendrons on the lawn's edges were flapping their leaves so loud that they were on the verge of drowning the sound of the helicopter's rotor blades.

From the back of the house, Fernando Monterrey appeared through one of the large glass doors. For a moment he stood still, watching the machine descend the last few meters.

"I'm sorry, Catherine," he mumbled. "I never meant you to harm you."

Then the old man bent over forward a little bit and walked right into the blazing wind from the helicopter.

He walked across the grass, stepped into the helicopter, sat down and fastened his seatbelt and then looked down on his beautiful home, the place that had failed to free him from his past. He saw a young Catherine Gretta in front of him, how she laughed and danced, a queen of the past. A girl with the looks of a film noir woman, sultry and in control. But she was not real and he knew it; what he saw in his mind's eye was a projection of a woman. Because by now he had forgotten what she really looked like and he had destroyed all photographs of her forever ago.

Then the image disappeared and there was only this situation, this thing that was about to explode and go public.

Go public — the one thing that both he and Catherine had been trying to avoid for so long.

Twenty-four

It looks so easy in the movies, Carl Pappas thought.

He tried to think of all the actors he had seen crawling on top of a fast-moving train. Sean Connery? Bruce Willis? Harrison Ford? Jon Voight? Or was it only a blundering Peter Sellers, falling off it? He couldn't remember a single scene from a single movie, nor could he remember any tactics involved that might come in handy at this particular moment.

For he was lying flat on one of the freight train's wagon roofs, with absolutely nothing to hold on to, while the wind jerked at him continuously and his fingers were getting really numb from the cold. He was afraid that if he'd move, he'd fall off.

Twelve wagons separated him from the locomotive where Catherine Gretta was. Or should be.

"How come you're not moving?" the Lieutenant shouted from behind him.

The bizz jockey wanted to answer "You go first" but he swallowed that remark. He slowly got up to a frog position and made small steps towards the back of the train. There, behind them all, was the locomotive.

"If he looks above the train, he'll spot us immediately," he shouted.

"We have no choice. He can't throw explosives this far anyway."

"He may yet have a gun," shouted Carl.

"Ah! So you've changed your mind about that, bizz jockey!"

Catherine Gretta had gotten up and leaned against the dashboard, carefully covering the fifth monitor, the one that was showing the view of the camera on top of the train. She had spotted the two figures on top while her abductor was looking out one of the windows and decided to act.

Then suddenly he grabbed her purse.

"Sure," said Gretta. "So you're a purse snatcher as well. Have you no respect for a woman's privacy, man?"

He gave her back her purse and started dialing a number on her cell phone.

"Ah, I see," she said. "You need to get to your wife and inform her you'll be late for dinner. I hate to think about your kids and how she will have to raise them all by herself while you're stashed away in some heavy security prison in a faraway place, miles from the inhabited world, where no one will ever come to visit you."

"It's me," said the man into the phone. "What? I can't hear you. Listen, my battery has been gone all this time, I was hiding in the train, I thought I would simply sit this thing out, but all of a sudden I was trapped. It was now or never."

"You're fired," Catherine Gretta continued her monologue. "I can tell. There's no doubt about it, you can't talk your way out of this one."

"I can't hear you!" shouted the man. "Listen, you have to think of something or else..."

"You are undoubtedly not very clever," said Gretta. "You've completely improvised this escape, haven't you? You were safe in this train until you jumped on me. Nobody knew you were here and now the whole world is looking at you..."

"You want me to whát? ... Hello? ... You want me to stop? Are you insane?"

Fernando Monterrey was finally put through to the cell phone of the police chief in charge of the whole operation. It had taken quite a while, but now that he was talking to the responsible officer, he had to be very convincing and keep himself out of the loop.

"I can make the train stop," he said, "and negotiate a safe way out for the hostage for you."

"Who the hell are you?" barked the chief. "Do you know the terrorist?"

"Yes I do," said Monterrey. "To make sure my intentions are good, I have arranged for the train to stop exactly twelve minutes from now. Just make sure the police force stays away for another half hour. I will call you then to inform you of the status."

"You will have to be more specific than that," said the police chief. "You want me to stay back until you, an unidentified person connected to the crime, takes care of things?"

"It doesn't matter either way," said Monterrey. "If you approach the train just like that, the hostage might die." Then he disconnected the call.

All of a sudden he felt nauseous. What have I done, he thought. I've created a living nightmare that's put Catherine in a deadly situation. I should never have hired that idiot, that fool. What had he been thinking, trying to escape by freight train with the whole world watching?

He looked at his phone. It was an unregistered number he had switched to for this purpose only.

He opened the window slightly and threw it out.

Now that he had used it to call the police, he'd better not carry it with him.

Again he felt pain take over.

"What puzzles me, my dear man," said Catherine, "are the explosives you've put in my dry sachets. How much stuff is there?"

"About a hundred, maybe more," said the man.

"Oh my. There's going to be a hundred explosions in the coming days?"

"There's also the stuff I got here," he added. He pointed at a bag he was carrying across his shoulders. "Enough to blow this entire loc to smithereens," he said, "so you better be a good old lady."

On the roof, Lieutenant Carlsberg looked at a text message on his cell phone.

Then he turned his head towards Carl Pappas — which was quite difficult since they were both lying on their stomachs on the roof of the train and Pappas was behind him — and shouted: "The train will stop in a couple of minutes. It seems to be some kind of intervention. That'll give us a window of opportunity. Let's move forward quickly."

The Lieutenant started to crawl forward again and didn't notice what the bizz jockey was saying behind him.

"You're going to attack that terrorist yourself? So there's no all-powerful anti terrorist squad coming down from choppers to kick ass here? I can't believe it. You're in the same shape as I am, which means you have a lousy condition, your physical reflexes have deteriorated over the years and you overestimate yourself."

For a moment the bizz jockey felt for his cell phone, but the movements of the train were too powerful — he quickly put back the hand flat on the roof and started to follow the Lieutenant.

"Our only chance is to talk the man out of it," he continued, but he realized the policeman in front of him wasn't hearing him.

Twenty-five

The landscape was deserted except for the freight train. The massive hulk was slowing down rapidly in an endless ocean of low hills, mostly covered with low bushes. There was no way a police force could be close to the train and remain unseen at the same time. Beyond the hills there was no sign of anything flying.

The brakes where doing their work. There was a lot of bumping and clattering and smoke curling upwards. By then Pappas and Carlsberg had reached the locomotive roof and had a hard time holding on.

It was only when the train had come to a complete halt that the bizz jockey and the Lieutenant noticed the sound of the helicopter. It came roaring over a hill towards the locomotive and set down on the rails behind it.

It all happened very fast. On the left of the locomotive, they heard a door open, while from the helicopter a tall man, probably in his sixties, emerged and started walking fast towards the train.

Carl saw Carlsberg crawl to the right side of the locomotive's roof. Then he looked back and gestured towards the bizz jockey. Pappas got the message and grabbed the Lieutenant's ankles. That allowed the policeman to push his upper torso, or most of it, over the edge and do something out of the bizz jockey's sight.

Then all of a sudden there was a lot of movement and Carl had a few tough moments as a lot of weight pulled at his hands and by the time he had the nerve to look up again, he saw Catherine Gretta crawl onto the roof, aided by Carlsberg.

Without talking, the three of them ran over the roof, made it across to the first wagon and continued running.

Behind them there was some shouting, muffled from under the roof, and then the train started moving again.

"This ain't right," shouted Carl. "We have to get off before the train goes too fast again."

But Carlsberg just kept running, going down after each carriage to help Mrs. Gretta climb down and up again, moving further and further towards the front of the freight train.

In the distance they could hear the helicopter taking off again.

"What on earth are you doing!" shouted Fernando Monterrey, when the terrorist hit the dashboard and got the train moving again. "You are just making things worse. Let me go after them and..."

"They are not getting off this train while it is moving," said the terrorist. "She's an old woman, they won't take the risk."

"And then whát? Listen, you have to turn yourself in. You will jump off the train and hide, and I will tell the police something, well, I have come up with a story they'll swallow. They have given me a half hour to sort this out. But if we don't act now, they'll show up and then we will both be facing the music"

"So, you've been talking to the police? That sucks."

"If it weren't for me, they would have attacked you already, don't you understand? You're putting the life of Catherine Gretta on the line here."

"Well, you sent me off to disrupt her business and that's exactly what I'm doing, so why the big mouth?"

Fernando Monterrey was at his wit's end. He now realized that he had hired a ruthless criminal, someone who was quite happy to let things escalate the way they were.

"You were hired to trigger a few minor explosions that would bring the Desi stock down," shouted Monterrey. "Not hijack a train and kidnap Mrs. Gretta and have the entire police force on your trail."

"Well, your precious Desi stock should be making a massive nosedive by now," retorted the terrorist sarcastically, "so what's your problem?"

"Because I still love Cath..." Fernando shut his mouth as soon as he realized his mistake, but it was too late.

The terrorist just looked at him in a pitiful way. "I'm sure glad you paid me in advance," he said. "You're one crazy son of a bitch. I got me in all this trouble for love?"

Twenty-six

There was a dead man in the wagon. Or so it seemed.

Pappas, Carlsberg and Gretta — surprisingly agile for a woman her age — had climbed down between the two carriages that formed the front of the long freight train, and entered. In the half-light they saw a man lying on the wooden floor, between crates, all tied up and a scarf tied around his mouth.

But then the man moved and opened his eyes and Mrs. Gretta shrieked. "Good heavens," she said, and kneeled down to remove the scarf.

Meanwhile Lieutenant Carlsberg started to remove the rope around his hands, that were tied to his back.

Carl looked at the crates. "Gosh just see how many dry sachets are being shipped into the world," he said. "I knew the numbers, but actually seeing the motherload is quite a different story."

"Are you all right, Mr. Bremen?" said Carlsberg.

"I seem to be alive," the man said. "But that's about it. I thought I was going to die of thirst. That... that lunatic held me here for days."

"Speak no further, my dear man," said Mrs. Gretta. Then she turned to Carlsberg. "This man needs medical attention and get him some water as fast as possible."

"We'll all be needing medical attention very soon if we're not getting outside help," said Carlsberg as he got his cell phone out again and started dialing.

"I sure hope you guys are coming," said Carlsberg. "That intervention clearly didn't work. What was that about anyway?" He listened for a while and then put the cell phone away. "They're in pursuit of the train right now," he said to his companions.

There was a sudden jerk and they all stumbled to the left side of the wagon, except for John Bremen, who was still sitting down. Mrs. Gretta fell on her back.

An army jet roared over the train, made a circular movement and flew over it again.

In the distance, five helicopters were approaching rapidly. Two bore army colors, two were from the police force and one carried the WCBN Radio colors.

Carlsberg, hanging from the side door of the wagon, looked up and shouted back inside: "There they are. Everybody lie down in the middle of the wagon. We could be in for a rough ride."

While they were doing that, the bizz jockey said: "Wouldn't it be better if we tried to jump off while we still can?"

"At this speed? Out of the question!"

In the sky, Hitomi Sakamoto and Phil Solo looked down from the WCBN Radio helicopter.

"I'd say they're going way too fast!" shouted Solo, trying to make himself heard above the roar of the rotor blades.

"Can't you call Carlsberg and ask what's going on?" answered Hitomi.

"Ás if he's going to tell me anything I don't already know!"

Then they heard the pilot's voice through the helicopter speaker system. "The train is derailing!"

A cold hand gripped their hearts as they watched the wagons start to leave the track, one by one, a long snake trying to find another way through the landscape. In its wake it pulled a cloud of dust from the ground like a working volcano — the last thing they saw in this upcoming rain of ash and bush shrapnel was the curling and jumping and tipping over of the snake.

Explosions started to rip through the noise of the helicopter blades.

Twenty-seven

By the time the WCBN Radio helicopter had set down on a small open space in the bushy terrain, the cloud had dispersed from almost the entire freight train. Only the locomotive was still hidden by billowing smoke. A fire was raging within, and every now and then a new explosion could be heard.

Men from the army helicopters stood close and tried to extinguish the fire and the explosions with synthetic foam. Every explosion jettisoned new glass and metal into the air, keeping Hitomi and Phil inside the helicopter until all the noise had stopped.

Then they pushed open the side door and rushed out.

"There's Carlsberg over there!" shouted Hitomi. "Let's see if Carl's with him."

"And Catherine," panted Solo. He was a man who worked out, so he could take a little excitement, but he still couldn't keep up with Miss Sakamoto. There and then he decided that this was unacceptable.

Close to the first wagon, that lay on its side, stood the bizz jockey and the Lieutenant and the factory foreman and the

Desi owner, among the bushes. The settling dust gave them the appearance of ghosts.

When they got to the scene, Hitomi embraced the bizz jockey and her boss embraced Catherine Gretta. This left the other two men standing there, John Bremen and Lieutenant Carlsberg, with nothing much to do.

Carlsberg took this all in and tried to come up with a suitable wisecrack.

But John Bremen beat him to it. "That's all right," he said while he shrugged. "I haven't been very popular lately anyway. I'm sort of getting used to it."

To that, Mrs. Gretta smiled, freed herself from Phil Solo, stepped forward and embraced the battered foreman of her factory. "My good man," she said. "We were on the same train."

When Carl saw Carlsberg look at Hitomi, he copied Mrs. Gretta's gesture by stepping forward to embrace the Lieutenant. "That goes for you too, detective."

"I'm a Lieutenant, bizz jockey."

Then Carlsberg almost fainted and went limb in the bizz jockey's arms. "Hitomi, help me here," said Carl.

Hitomi rushed to her boss, helping the shocked Lieutenant to sit down on the ground. "But... you're bleeding, Mr. Detective," she said, appalled at the dark red spots on his uniform blouse, that became visible when his jacket slipped open.

The policeman answered with a grunt, that appeared to be coming from his deepest inside.

"Go get help," said Mrs. Gretta to John Bremen. "Hurry, man." Then she held his arm. "Unless you're wounded as well.

Let me check."

They looked on as the old lady glanced up and down her foreman, approved of his condition and sent him off.

"You are the toughest of everybody who's present, by a long shot, Mrs. Gretta," said Pappas.

"I have a guardian angel, no doubt. Don't flatter me, Mr. Bizz Jockey, I bumped my head. I may be in for the final concussion of my life."

Then a voice came hollering out of nowhere: "Hitomi. What are you doing here?"

"Not again," said the bizz jockey. But he didn't rotate his eyes; he just smiled.

It was Moon Afficionades, who walked towards them, accompanied by two security men in fittingly dark suits.

"Official business," said Hitomi, as she exchanged air kisses with the young man. "Let me guess: your family owns the freight company."

"And the railway, actually," said Moon. He held Hitomi by both her shoulders, looked her up and down and nodded. Then he moved about to shake hands.

When he came to Mrs. Gretta, he said: "Catherine. I heard. What a terrible ordeal. My dad says anything we can do. Anything. Just whistle."

"I'm fine, young man."

"Who was this lunatic?"

"That's a long story. Undoubtedly I'm in for long sessions in the courtroom, I fear."

"Don't fear, Mrs. Gretta," said Moon. "Not anymore, that is."

They all looked towards the end of the train, where the

smoking remains of the locomotive were.

"Why?" said Catherine.

"Both men are... well, they're gone. There's nothing left of them. They tell me the explosive dry sachets they were carrying blew them apart when the train went off the track."

Hitomi sat down with Lieutenant Carlsberg and tried to comfort him in his agony, for the pain was obviously starting to get to him. Moon also kneeled. The bizz jockey looked on as his producer tried to divide her attention equally between the two men.

She has this strange effect on men, he thought. One is faking death throes and the other is trying to impress her with all his family's worldly possessions once again.

At last arrangements were being made for the evacuation of the wounded Lieutenant in the Afficionades' corporate helicopter. They took off with the policeman on a stretcher, accompanied by Moon Afficionades.

"We're taking a police car," said Hitomi to Carl. "I don't feel like flying again."

"I'll fly," said Catherine Gretta to Phil Solo. "I want to get out of here before the press arrives."

"Follow me," said Solo. "I have a helicopter waiting too."

When they were alone at last, Carl Pappas started to beat the dust off his jacket and pants. "Enough with all this, Hitomi. Let's talk to whoever's in charge of this and see what's being done about the remaining dry sachets of death from the factory. Heaven knows how many of them are still at large."

Twenty-eight

The roof garden had been there as long as the building itself. Which must have been decades at least. Like the worn, weathered and darkened sandstones, the trees and bushes were showing their age. It gave the place character; being there gave Philemon Solo the distinct feeling that many generations of powerful people had looked down on the city from this terrace, in times of war and peace, talked about it, and then forgotten it again. And now he was standing here with Catherine Gretta, another member of the small circle of famous people — albeit only in the memories of older people. Those who were old enough to remember her days as a starlet. But she had been quite agile in erasing her past; she had evaded the limelight for decades.

That period of her life seemed to be drawing to a close.

"Do you regret that you'll be at the center of attention once again?" said Phil Solo.

They stood at the far end of the roof garden, where they could see the city bathed in the evening light. The temperature was soft and the stars added a movie-like backdrop.

"It's all too crazy to contemplate," said Catherine. "You know how the British value keeping up appearances? I think I will approach it in that spirit: simply deal with it in an appropriate manner"

"So, what's appropriate in this case, then?"

"I haven't figured that out yet, Philemon. Tomorrow I will negotiate with your bizz jockey and see if I want to be on The Boardroom. If I play this right, I can make my statements there and satisfy the entire media circus in a single shot. The Boardroom is the highest profile media spot, there's nothing beyond it."

"Thank you for the compliment."

"I wasn't giving one. My, your ego is alive. Has anyone ever told you that, Mr. WCBN Radio executive?" But without giving him a chance to answer, she walked to a table and switched on a radio.

It was a strange place for a radio, but it was also a strange occasion, of course.

"What are you doing?" said Phil Solo.

"You are the boss of the bizz jockey, you said you always listen to his show no matter what. Well, it's starting. I think we should listen."

Phil smiled.

While Catherine poured red wine in two glasses, a voice came from the radio and made conversation needless for a moment.

"And... it's eleven o'clock. The city is dark, but the fire burns. It burns in the offices. It burns on Wall Street. It burns in the City. It burns on the Bund. It burns in Dubai. It burns in the factories and power plants. And it burns within us.

Because we are the business and we all need redemption. This is the hour of delusion and today's truth. This is The Boardroom. Here is your prophet, the buddy and the bodyguard of every CEO, the Don Juan of every business babe. Here is the world's one and only bizz jockey. Here is your BJ: Carl Pappas!"

They touched glasses.

"I hope you people have been paying attention these past few days, because some of you are in real danger. There's still fourteen dry sachets missing from the Desi disaster. So for once in your lives, get in gear and call me if you have purchased a new computer bag or a rucksack in the past seven days. It may explode in your face before this show is over. We don't want that to happen. So get to the boardroom dot com and hit the dial button. My producer Hitomi Sakamoto is ready for some serious action."

They drank.

"Here's a quick update to begin with. In the studio is Lieutenant Carlsberg. What's the status, Lieutenant?"

"We could discover the exact quantity of explosives the terrorist placed in the Desi factory. Much of the missing stuff has turned up thanks to the general public. Lots of people responded quickly to our instructions and so many lives have been saved."

"Why did this man do this in the first place?"

"I've promised the people involved I wouldn't speak about that just now. But I understand someone else will be later," said Carlsberg.

"Actually, that's quite right," said Pappas. "Tomorrow, Mrs. Catherine Gretta will appear in The Boardroom and explain how this all came to be. But tonight I will be talking to the CEO and the foreman of the Desi Corporation, because they are announcing.... the end of the strike!"

"So they've made peace."

"They have indeed."

In the roof garden, Catherine Gretta said: "That bizz jockey of yours, he talks an awful lot, doesn't he?"

Phil Solo shrugged. "I guess so. More than average, at the very least. But that's also precisely what makes him such a fine investment for the owners of WCBN Radio."

Catherine shot him a gloomy look, one he had a hard time interpreting as serious or ironic.

"I wouldn't want my investments talking back to me. I want them to make a neat profit in perfect silence."

From the radio, the voice of Carl Pappas became audible again. "By the way, I've been talking to a lot of strikers these days. One of them told me that he came home from a strike and found his wife in the bedroom, all powdered up and stuff. She was wearing designer clothing from New York. 'Why are you smelling and dressing like we're going to a party,' he says, 'while I am going through hell?' So his wife says: 'I just want to cheer you up, honey.' And he says: 'What'd you pay for these clothes?' And she says: 'Well, about the amount you are going to get for a raise once your strike is successful.'"

There was a mild laugh from Lieutenant Carlsberg on the other side of the radio studio table, but it was obvious that in the roof garden nobody was listening anymore.

A tall man in his late thirties, impeccably dressed, his hair combed back, was kissing a beautiful lady in her mid sixties, wearing a red robe and her hair in a knot, her pearl necklace glistening in the light from the roof candles. Behind them, a butler refilled their glasses and switched the radio to a station broadcasting soft jazz, giving Carl Pappas, the bizz jockey, a deadly verdict.

***

Request from the author

Thank you for reading this Radio Detective adventure. I hope you enjoyed it and will be willing to write a review on the platform of your choice, like Amazon, Apple iBooks, Kobo or Goodreads. Making that extra effort is greatly appreciated by other readers... and of course by me. Thank you.

I hope you and I stay connected through Twitter, Facebook, Google+, Pinterest or my free email newsletter. I'll make sure you'll stay tuned.

Have a good evening/night/day!

M.H. Vesseur

Twitter @MHVesseur

Facebook www.facebook.com/MHVesseur

Subscribe to M.H. Vesseur's mailing list on www.mhvesseur.com

About the author

M.H. Vesseur has written many short stories for literary magazines in The Netherlands, Belgium, Canada and the U.S.A. He was awarded for the best debut with his first story. In his radio detective series about Carl Pappas he has now written and published the seven short crime novels *CEO Groupie*, *Die Rich*, *Tax Me If You Can*, *Acid Asset*, *Nosedive*, *Power Play* and *Blood Border*. The radio detective's producer Hitomi Sakamoto now stars in her own series, which begins with *North*. M.H. Vesseur also published the novel *Lemniscate*, a collection of literary short stories called *Allusions* and his outlook on the super economy *Burning Neil Armstrong*. M.H. Vesseur is an awarded advertising copywriter. He lives in the forests of The Netherlands.

www.mhvesseur.com

Novels and ebooks by M.H. Vesseur

You can find links to online stores on:
www.mhvesseur.com/publications

Allusions (short story collection)
North (The Hitomi Files: 1)
Blood Border (a Radio Detective novel)
Power Play (a Radio Detective novel)
Nosedive (a Radio Detective novel)
Acid Asset (a Radio Detective novel)
Tax Me If You Can (a Radio Detective novel)
Die Rich (a Radio Detective novel)
CEO Groupie (a Radio Detective novel)
Beloved Stalker
Babyface Junkie
In Snuff Park
Sketches Of A Worldwide Christo And Jeanne-Claude
Narcissist Guru
Territory Game

Short stories by M.H. Vesseur

Ebook en paperback bij Amazon, ebook bij Apple iBooks en Kobo

ALLUSIONS

Glimpses of tomorrow await you in this collection. The ultimate amusement park will offer you death. Everlasting youth will take you to the point of no return. The artificial landscape will fill you with joy if it doesn't scare the living daylights out of you. The Narcissist Guru will show you your many selves. There is the ultimate work of art that will change the planet and the old vaudeville star who is still being stalked. And finally, the coming of the super economy will haunt your dreams. This collection contains the short stories • In Snuff Park • Babyface Junkie • Narcissist Guru • Sketches of a Worldwide Christo and Jeanne-Claude • Territory Game • Beloved Stalker • Burning Neil Armstrong.

Available in The Hitomi Files by M.H. Vesseur

Ebooks and paperback, on Amazon, Apple iBooks and Kobo

NORTH

Man should fear only one enemy

The only enemy who has the capacity to remove all of mankind from the earth, is the virus. Imagine the worst of them all, a true 21st century killer. It lies dormant in the remote laboratory of a pharmaceutical giant whose hopes of making billions off a vaccine somewhere in the future throw a dark shadow ahead. Then Hitomi Sakamoto, the hard boiled radio producer who's on a rough vacation in the wild nature of the north, stumbles upon this dark secret. She is drawn into a final battle between ruthless scientists, a greedy corporation, desperate but dangerous environmental activists, a cold-hearted assassin and... a manmade virus that longs to escape.

Hitomi Sakamoto first appeared in the Radio Detective novels by M.H. Vesseur. Immediately popular for her iron work ethics and razorsharp tongue, Hitomi outgrew her boss (radio detective Carl Pappas) and now steps out of his shadow, into her very own adventure.

Available in the radio detective series by M.H. Vesseur

Ebook and paperback in the Amazon Store

CEO GROUPIE - A radio detective novel

One night three live guests join Carl Pappas on his radio show The Boardroom: two CEOs and a woman who calls herself: "the CEO Groupie". When the mysterious woman reveals the existence of a secret call girl organization for CEOs and subsequently disappears a couple of days later, the bizz jockey engages on a search. What happened to the CEO Groupie and what are the other two guests up to? Together with his radio team — his producer Hitomi Sakamoto and his sound engineer Don Wozniak — Carl Pappas sets out to deal with this.

Available in the radio detective series by M.H. Vesseur

Ebook and paperback in the Amazon Store

DIE RICH - A radio detective novel

Carl Pappas, the bizz jockey, goes on the air again. His radio show "The Boardroom" is both loved and feared by the global business community. He has a sharp eye for business news and the big mouth of a talk radio host. This time around he has some very wealthy guests joining him on his show: two billionaire entrepeneurs and their future successors, who also happen to be their sons. Of course it doesn't take the bizz jockey a very long time to upset some of his guests and his audience — and that same night the bizz jockey finds himself heading into dangerous waters, in the hands of some very angry rich people. His team — producer Hitomi Sakamoto and sound engineer Don Wozniak — is forced to go out and rescue their reckless boss. And then there are the rich kids they have to deal with...

Available in the radio detective series by M.H. Vesseur

Ebook and paperback in the Amazon Store

ACID ASSET - A radio detective novel

Carl Pappas, the bizz jockey, is feeling good about the prospects of environment-friendly plastics he's discussing on his radio show "The Boardroom". But as he soon finds out there's something not right with the company behind it. Can the bizz jockey protect a lonely scientist against the schemes of a large corporation that smells money? Or will he be unable to stop a revolutionary asset from becoming really acidic? Buckle up for a race against arsonists, corporate crime, dogs, bullets and a dangerous industrial zone in the middle of a blizzard, softened only by some real team spirit.

Available in the radio detective series by M.H. Vesseur

Ebook and paperback in the Amazon Store

POWER PLAY - A radio detective novel

The death of an environmental activist brings bizz jockey and unofficial "radio detective" Carl Pappas to the quiet island of Islasol. Everything seems to be OK with the local National Park and the wind turbine park in the heart of it.

But Carl and his team soon find out you can't take anything on face value. Below the surface of an environment friendly enterprise lies a darker secret. It's time for the radio detective to unravel the local secrets of wind energy, assisted by his producer Hitomi and a new, unlikely ally.

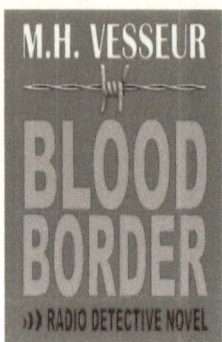
<<<<>>>>